OUT OF THE DARKNESS

A Collection of Dark Fantasy Tales

AMPHIBIAN PRESS

This is a work of fiction. All of the characters, organizations, and events portrayed in this novel are either products of the author's imagination or are used fictitiously.

OUT OF THE DARKNESS

Copyright © 2017 by Sara Voorhis

Amphibian Press
www.amphibianpressbooks.com

ISBN :   9780998333229

First Edition

Table of Contents

Foreword

I first had the privilege to read these stories when I was in Europe, trying to outrun my seasonal sadness. I dove into them on a particularly rainy day, frustrated that I couldn't go outside, run, shake off my bad feelings, or really go anywhere besides my makeshift desk that was my mother-in-law's couch.

"It's the weather," I tell everyone as to why early spring so frequently brings me to my knees. But, in reality, I wonder if it has more to do with the world waking up long before it's ready to be green again. The stillness of winter is gone, but you can't yet run outside and throw your arms up to the sun, breathing in the vibrancy around you. You have to wait for the snow to turn to mud and the budding grass to battle those last few ice storms (if you're in New England, anyway) before you get your prize of flowering trees and beaches.

During this time, my own ambitions unfreeze, as does the anxiety that goes with them.

"Let's travel next spring," my husband gently suggested last year as I sobbed into my pillow. So we bought tickets to Holland and hopped on a plane, hoping that warmer weather and a change of scenery would do the trick. But, while friends, food, and language challenges kept the worst of my yearly spiral at bay, his hometown has a penchant for rain.

So, on that early April morning as the clouds poured their contents onto the city, I thought to myself, what better to read than an anthology promising to bring me Out of the Darkness? I opened this book and began to read.

Fantasy, as a genre, is frequently seen as an escape. The problems of the real word are shoved away in favor of magic, gods, heroes, and made-up kingdoms. The magnitude of the difficulties that the characters face help put our own lives in perspective, and make the real world seem more manageable. That's always been the view from the outside, anyway, but those of us who frequent the genre know better.

Instead of finding unrealistic adventures that would make me forget my real life for a second, I found stories of strength, pain, and choices that opened and broke my heart over and over again. I found the agony that comes from not ever belonging. I found how nearly impossible it can be to succeed when it means that others fail. I found a man who tapped into his own power only after he'd lost everything. And I found sisters fighting for each other in a broken world.

As I lay on that couch and tore through these tales, I realized that the world around me wasn't vanishing, it was changing. I hadn't outrun the discomfort of my own fears for the future, I had gone to a place where I knew I could better face them.

These stories are not an escape. Nothing about them will put you at ease, or make you forget the darkness that flickers at the edges, and sometimes the core, of reality. These writers did not sit down and create a story to take your mind off things. They wrote these stories to fight.

Fantasy is not a genre of escape, it is a genre of confrontation. It's a genre that allows you to think outside your usual toolbox and imagine all the ways you could become more than you are. Fantasy writers frequently feel the real world more deeply than anyone else, and that is why they craft new worlds. We are lucky enough that four such authors have chosen to share their stories with us.

In these stories, you will find challenges bigger, stronger, and more heart-wrenching than you will ever face. The restrictions have been lifted and the worst can, and does, happen. But with these challenges come strength, resourcefulness, and the drive to move forward, to win, and to stay alive. And through reading these stories, you will find that, too.

You won't be lifted out of darkness. You'll fight your way there. And you'll create your own light.

So, dear reader, I urge you to take this journey. Let your problems get so big that they fill the entire sky, and the find the power to beat them. Let these authors open up to you in a way that is entirely fictional, and entirely real. Let yourself move from world to world and learn about the different ways these heroes move ahead.

I promise you, it will be worth it.

- Amy Spitzfaden

HOW TO CURSE A KINGDOM

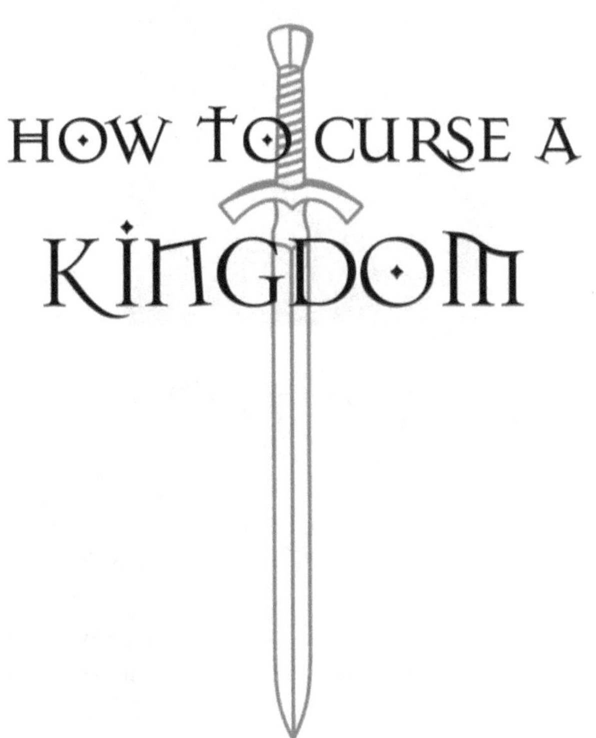

CAMERON J. QUINN

About Cameron J. Quinn

Cameron Quinn is an author of Paranormal Romance, Horror, Urban Fantasy, and Thriller genres. The first season of The Starsboro Chronicles, a series of ten Urban Fantasy novelettes will be completed in 2017.

She works as the Head of Marketing at Amphibian Press; a small press dedicated to helping independent authors navigate the publishing ocean. Her home is in central New England with her husband, three children, and too many animals to mention, but she hopes to travel a bit before truly settling down.

She can be found on her website as well as Facebook, Twitter, Goodreads, and Instagram.

www.cameronquinnbooks.com

How to Curse a Kingdom

Armon lay on the cool smooth stones of the riverbank. The blue sun bathing him in a warm glow as dark clouds threatened to ruin the day on the horizon.

Lightning flashed and thunder rolled over the fields and through the trees towards him. The dragons nearby stopped in their afternoon routines to listen. Armon's father was not the most subtle god in the pantheon. This was Dios' way of letting his son know he was not pleased.

Armon closed his eyes and placed a black scaled hand in the running water. The cool softness of the current relaxing him in a way few things could. His father was always upset with him about something.

You'd think I'd be used to it by now. The thought, as familiar as the pit in his stomach.

Whatever the ruler of the Gods wanted, it would have to wait. Armon wasn't ready to return to Taivas. He was the God of War and Chaos after all. Taivas could use a little chaos.

The clouds rolled in, lightening sending the baby dragons scurrying to their mothers as the sky opened up.

Armon didn't mind the rain normally, but this wasn't nature. This with his father's temper tantrum.

He sat up, his gaze following the river back towards the elven city of Taliz. He'd always wanted to see inside the palace.

The Flacari kingdom was by far his favorite, but Taliz, the capital city, held a special place in his heart. The people were kind and accepting for the most part. He had to hide his true form, with a thought his scales were replaced by the Flacari's tawny flesh. His eyes turned from blood red to a pale green and his wings and tail vanished. Around the dragons he fit in, but they were poor conversationalist. Armon's black and red scales were unsettling even among the Gods where he grew up. He'd learned early on how to disguise himself to fit in with the elves. His transformation was pure magic. If someone were to touch him they would feel only the soft skin of an elf. The disguise would vanish if he fell asleep, though.

He watched as his hand turned from a scaled claw into a smooth tanned fist. The transformation flowed over him, hiding his abnormalities from the world. His mother insisted he was beautiful and the elves would worship him as they do his father but the truth was, when they looked at him, fear filled their eyes. Not that he blamed them. Most of the gods were bright, beautiful colors. He was black with red swirls throughout, had bat-like wings and a tail that could rival a dragons. Of course, he suspected it was his pupil-less blood red eyes that scared them the most.

Choosing to think of other things, he walked along the stream toward the city. He could see the palace from this vantage point. The elves that called this place home carved it out of the stone of the volcano centuries ago. He'd heard that there was a passage leading into the belly of the volcano. It was rumored that the kings would toss their enemies in as well as criminals convicted of the most severe crimes. His cousin, Draxis, the god of fire, claimed they made sacrifices to him there.

Curiosity propelled Armon forward and before long he found himself weaving through the city streets and markets until he was at the foot of the great staircase that lead into the palace. Despite his powers, he had never been in the palace before. He spent most of his downtime near the market or the pier watching the common elves go about their day. Royals were a bit stuck up for his taste. Today, however, he wanted to see the inside of the volcano.

He stood, silently admiring the architecture as the hustle and bustle of city life went on around him. The structure was rough and yet somehow beautiful. If he ever built his own temple back home in the God's Realm, Taivas, he'd model it after this.

With a simple thought he disappeared from the view of the elves and slipped up the grand staircase and into the palace. Sticking to shadows, he explored, following maids and errand boys. Stopping by the War Room when we came across it. He was the God of War and Destruction after all.

The room was like most, with maps and charts covering the walls and a large rock formation at its center. The rock had been carved out in the center to hold water, which could be manipulated by certain elves to take on maps and battlefields for strategizing.

Feeling unimpressed, he was about to leave when two men entered.

"Where is the King?" one asked looking around at the seemingly empty room.

"He's trying to get that new wife of his to obey," the other responded with a laugh.

Armon frowned.

"She's something else. A real fighter that one," the first man said. "If he gets her to comply, she'll bear him many strong sons."

"And a beautiful daughter he can use to gain power in another kingdom."

Armon glared. He'd never understood some men's inability to see a woman's worth.

Disgusted, and making a point to see this king fail in battle sooner rather than later, he slipped out the door. To the left was the direction he'd come from and the right held a dark narrow staircase.

He was about to retire to the dragons when a scream filtered down from somewhere upstairs. Armon took off up the stairs before he could think better of it. The terrified sounds got louder and louder as he neared the top level. The woman was screaming in anger and demanding her attacker to stop. When Armon reached the large ornate door he pushed through with his shoulder.

A man was on top of the woman on the bed, struggling to spread her legs as he pulled down his pants. Based on their attire this was the couple the man in the war room spoke of.

The man paused long enough to see who had entered. "Get out," he snapped.

The woman was silent as tears fell from her eyes. Armon grabbed the man by his shoulder and shoved him to the floor.

The man shot to his feet pulling up his pants as he went.

"I've put elves to death for less than that," he said puffing out his chest. Armon stifled a laugh as he put himself between the man and the bed.

"You wouldn't be the first," Armon said with smile. "I'm certain my father would have drowned me at birth, if I could be killed."

The man looked confused. Armon stepped forward, allowing his natural red eyes to shine through his disguise and locked gazes with the king. "Leave, do not come here again unless expressly asked by the lady. Forget about me," he whispered. The King's eyes were vacant as he left the room muttering an apology. Armon wasn't supposed to mess with free will; he wasn't *supposed* to interfere with them elves at all.

"Thank you," the woman said. He turned to face her and frowned at him. He found himself staring. She looked so familiar. "Bahn?"

Recognition hit him at the name. he'd given it to her after rescuing her and a small group of travelers from the dragons a few months ago. After the rescue she'd tried to repay him with her body. He'd refused. That was one complication he did not need.

"Nicitiva." He looked around the room. "You never told me your business in Taliz was to become Queen."

"I was still hoping it wouldn't happen," she admitted before sitting up urgency burning in her burgundy eyes. "But you should not have done that. Do you know who that was?"

"Does it matter?" he asked as he set about fixing the door. The sooner it was fixed the sooner he'd be able to leave.

"If you value your life it does."

"Well, I don't." He winced. His life was not something he cared to preserve. Still, hearing it made it more real, somehow.

"Come here," she commanded. Armon gave a sigh. She was the Queen. He hated complications and she was as complicated as they came.

He approached the bed and she eyed him like a piece of sweet chew that children enjoyed. "You could be killed. I'm serious. You cannot threaten the king and you certainly cannot stop him from having his queen."

"You didn't seem to want what he was offering."

"That doesn't matter," she said. Another truth that made him flinch. "My father got very rich as a result of my marriage and it's my duty to deal with whatever that man wants."

Armon knew what she was trying to do, he didn't need her protection. He was done. He should stay out of the affairs of elves but he wasn't able to stand by while someone was being hurt. "Maybe next time you should take it quietly then."

Hurt shot across her face at his words and a pang of regret shot through his chest before he could dismiss it.

"I'll leave you to clean yourself up," he said as he turned to leave.

"Please don't go," she cried. "He'll come back if you go."

Armon thought about lying and staying with her but part of him refused the chance of being near something so beautiful for too long. "He will never come back here. Not unless you ask him."

She still looked terrified.

Armon pushed her out of his thoughts as he left. He was back at the stream before long and wondering why he bothered with elves at all. They were all so dramatic.

◆

Armon woke as a squabble broke out amongst the dragons. They were fighting over a scrap of meat. His body and soul were tired. All he wanted to do was roll over and go back to sleep but no sooner had the thought crossed his mind than one of the dragons hit him with its tail. The sharp tip sliced his back.

He let out a loud cry and both dragons stopped to look at him. He glared at them as he stood. Blood poured down his legs from the wound.

"Damn fool!" he roared at the dragon, who slipped away while the other snatched his prize and scuttled after.

Armon made his way to the market in search of a new shirt as the first of Ma Bet's three suns peeked over the mountains to the east.

Armon

His father's voice was like thunder in his head. He didn't respond as he continued on the path.

Armon, you need to come home. You cannot escape your duties forever.

He scoffed. His father had no idea what it was like up there. Even the Gods looked at him with fear or pity in their eyes. At least among the dragons he was accepted... for the most part.

His father had given up by the time he reached the market.

It was easily Armon's favorite place in the elven realm. It was beautiful and busy and no one noticed him. Just how he liked it.

He was haggling over a new shirt when he heard a screech. He turned slowly to see the Queen, Nicitiva, standing there looking aghast.

"Milady?"

"What happened to you?" she asked, as her disgust seemed to turn to concern.

"Got too close to a dragon. It looks worse than it is. Really."

"Come with me," she demanded, offering her hand. He stared at it for a long moment. He knew he should probably return to Taivas. But there was something in her eyes he couldn't resist. Something he'd rarely seen before. Kindness.

Back in the palace, she ordered Armon to remove his shirt and moved to examine the wound. It was likely almost healed by now. Dragons were one of the few creatures with the ability to hurt him and it always took longer for him to recover from their wounds.

He sat still as she poked and prodded his back. Supposedly cleaning the wound and preparing to sew it.

"This is nearly healed." He could hear the frown in her voice. "When did this happen?"

"I told you it wasn't as bad as it looked," he stood and put his new shirt on. He didn't want her to know who he was. She would demand to see his true form. He wanted to be a simple elf with her. Her equal and not something to be feared or worse, disgusted by.

"Don't run away." There was a hint of pleading in her voice. "I don't really know anyone here. I thought maybe we could talk."

He looked at her. She seemed so mystical sitting in her fine dress. Knowing it was a mistake; he turned the chair to face her and sat down.

A warm smile spilled across her face as she sat up.

"What did you want to talk about?" he asked.

"Why were you near dragons?" she asked settling in to listen to him. "You saved my party from them and now you're near them again. I would think you'd try and avoid the beasts."

"I prefer the company of dragons," he answered. He wasn't sure why he was telling her this. Some small part of him wanted her to know him. Even if she only knew a few pieces.

"What do you mean?"

"I live out there with them," he replied. "Dragons are amazing creatures. They don't fear you. And if you're very lucky, they will respect you."

"You crave respect?" she asked. She was curious.

"Yes." he decided to play along. It wasn't exactly the truth. He craved respect for being himself, not for being a god. And certainly not for being the most feared god in the pantheon. "What about you? What do you crave?"

"Freedom," she looked out the window as the light left her eyes and seriousness clouded her features.

"I always thought royals were the most free of the elves," he said. "I suppose you just have a slightly larger cage."

"One day," she started, still looking out the window, "women will be seen as equal, and no one will be forced to marry simply to fill their father's purse."

"Elves could learn something from the sachee in how they treat women."

"Sachee don't feel like we do, Bahn. They are savages. They just like to kill us and rape us."

"Kind of like your husband," Armon shot back before he could stop himself. She looked at the ground as they continued and he felt like an ass. "Look, they're just like you. They look a little different but cannot you see the beauty in that?"

"No," she said picking her head up. "I have a hard time looking past the sister they murdered trying to take over our home when I was a girl. I cannot seem to get past the things they did to my mother while I hid under the bed. Do you know what it's like to have your mother's blood drip through the mattress onto your face and not be able to scream?"

"War is ugly." He admitted. "But that does not mean all the people are ugly. Elves have done things to them that were just as bad. It does not excuse it. It's a fact. And when you get stuck on revenge and pain, you are the one who loses."

◆

Armon sat on the pier watching the sea birds try to steal fish from the fishermen. He didn't get joy from this anymore. He felt empty. Numb.

Someone tapped his shoulder and he turned to see a small boy staring up at him. He wore fine clothes and was cleaner than most living in Taliz. He was sent from the palace.

"Mr. Bahn?" he asked.

"Yes," Armon responded.

"The queen desires your presence sir," the boy gave him a small smile before running off toward the palace.

"Of course she does," he said mostly to himself. Still, there was something drawing him to her. Maybe it was the sadness behind her eyes. Or the way she seemed to want his friendship above all else. He wasn't sure.

He reached the palace and headed upstairs to her chambers. The door was ajar; he gave a slight nudge and it swung open. The room appeared empty. He stepped inside with a frown.

"Milady?"

The door shut behind him and he spun on his heel expecting the King to be there ready to try something foolish. What he found instead took his breath away. His eyes were wide as he stared at Nicitiva leaning against the door, completely naked. Her nipples were taught peaks on large breasts. His mouth watered at the sight. His eyes trailed down her body to the junction of her thighs. He'd never been with a woman before. He'd never felt comfortable. But seeing one naked, staring at him the way she did, made his body respond.

"I just wanted to apologize for how our last meeting ended. I know you were only there to appease me and I was not very gracious," she said, stepping towards him. Her words broke the spell her body had placed over him and he looked to the ceiling.

"Forgive me, I did not mean to stare."

"Is this not what you want?" she asked. She was close now. He could feel the heat of her body on his, though they weren't touching, yet. "I want you to do a lot more than stare."

"Milady, you're married."

"To an awful, pig of an elf. I've never wanted a man's touch the way I want yours. I burn for you." She pressed her body against his and it took all his self-control not to wrap his arms around her and take her to bed. "Hold me, Bahn."

She slid her hand down his breeches and wrapped her fingers around his manhood. "Just what I thought. You're hung like a god."

He looked into her burgundy eyes. She wanted him. She really wanted him. Giving into temptation he bent his head down to hers, capturing her lips with his. Wrapping his arms around her, he pulled her against him as she deepened the kiss. She let out an excited giggle as he picked her up and carried her to the bed.

He was a god, after all. What could go wrong?

◆

Armon lay in bed staring at Nicitiva. They'd been together many times over the past week. She couldn't seem to get enough of him. He'd never stop wanting her. She was the most beautiful thing he'd ever seen. Not like the gods and goddesses were beautiful back home. She had a different kind of grace. A different kind of beauty. Unique.

She sat, naked, on a cushioned chair with gold trimmings as she ran a brush through her honey colored hair. She hummed to herself, staring in the mirror. Picking out flaws he couldn't see despite her belief in their existence.

Armon? His mother's voice pulled him from his admiration. He groaned and rubbed a hand over his face.

What? His response was sharper than he intended.

Please come home. There was a hesitancy in her tone that filled him with regret.

Are you asking for you, or father?

For me, son. Please. I just want to talk.

He stood and looked around the room for his pants.

"Where are you going?" Nicitiva asked, a frown marring her features only slightly. "I'm not done with you yet."

"I have other responsibilities, my love."

"Like what? What could a peasant have to do that is more important than the queen's needs?"

"You have no idea what life is like outside these walls do you?" He smiled.

"I'll have you whipped," she teased.

"I'll be back as soon as I can," he gave her a chaste kiss on the cheek before pulling his tunic over his head and heading for the door.

Once in the hallway he shifted to his mother's gardens in Taivas. The only place in the world she would be without her husband. Sure enough, he found her near the waterfalls. A book lay forgotten in her lap. He took a moment to watch her. The goddess of growth and nature, her green skin held hints of blue and her short hair was a brilliant pink like the petals of a flower in the spring. He wished he'd been given half her beauty. He looked at his skin as it changed from the pale Flacari tones to the black scales with red swirls. His golden locks turned black and he knew his wings and horns were now visible. He hated the bat-like extensions. He was hideous. He ran his tongue over his teeth and cut it on his fangs. If he weren't completely himself she would worry. His mother thought he was beautiful. He knew himself to be something only a mother could love.

His mother looked away from the falls and a weak smile broke across her face.

"Hello, darling," she said extending her hand. He took it and allowed her to pull him to the water's edge.

"Mother," he said in greeting.

"Armon," she stressed his name so he waited for her to continue. "I have wonderful news."

He frowned. "What, is Stephini pregnant again?"

"No," she laughed. Her laugh always brightened his sour moods. He hated being here. Especially now. Knowing he would soon be returning for good. He couldn't ignore the people's suffering anymore. "We've found you a wife! The goddess of creation and balance."

"What?" His heart sank. No woman would want him. He couldn't force her just because he was the only god of war and destruction.

"You know the world of the gods is difficult. You cannot marry just anyone, and I'd lost hope that such a creature as her existed. But she's here and she's gorgeous, Armon. You'll love her I know it!"

"She'll faint as soon as she lays eyes on me, mother."

"You are meant to be. The Goddess of Creation and Balance and the God of War and Chaos. It was written in the stars. She is unique. Just like you. You owe it to yourself and to her to meet. To talk. Give her a chance."

"I will meet her, but I won't chase after her when she runs for cover."

"You are so dramatic."

◆

Armon stood behind the wall listening to his mother give his introduction. His heart beat so loudly in his chest he was sure they would hear it. He'd learned long ago people did not appreciate his visage.

"Armon?" his mother called. He willed his feet to move but they ignored him. She appeared around the corner. "Armon?"

"I'm trying."

"Not hard enough." She gripped his arm and yanked him into the room.

He looked at the floor waiting for the shrieks to begin. When silence met him, he looked up to see the goddess before him. Her white skin held black swirls as his held red. Her eyes were a ghostly white that filled him with unease. They held no pupils, giving no indication of where she was looking. She seemed as frightened of rejection as he felt. But she was beautiful.

"Hello," she said after a moment.

"Hello."

"Armon, this is Dematri."

"Delighted to meet you," she offered a slight smile.

"And you as well, Dematri." She looked away at his use of her full name and he wondered if he'd offended her somehow.

"I'll leave you two alone for a while." His mother stepped out of the room and Dematri looked back out the window.

"How do you...? Can we talk about..." his words drifted off.

"How do I feel about the idea of being married to someone I don't know?" she asked with a slight chuckle.

"I don't want you to feel that way. I know I'm difficult to look at. If you don't want me, just say the word and I can end this."

"You're hard to look at?" she asked. "You look fine to me."

He wondered if she was blind.

"I'm not blind, exactly." He jumped. Maybe she could read thoughts. "I can see truths, souls. And I can see thermals."

"You can see heat signatures?"

"Essentially."

He frowned. Maybe she was perfect for him. She couldn't see how hideous his physical appearance was. Maybe she would actually see him. He felt a smile curl his lips at the possibility of a friend. His first true friend. He held no delusions about Nicitiva. She would run screaming if she ever saw his true form.

"Where did you come from?" he asked.

"I was raised in the Mecusilik forest by the Sachee. They say I was born of fire and water but I never could get a real answer from them."

"You never met your parents?" Part of him envied that, but it was shoved aside by guilt. His mother loved him unconditionally. Knowing her was more than worth putting up with his father.

"Nope," she looked around the room seemingly content to be here. "What about you? You grew up here?"

"Yes," He didn't really want to talk about his childhood but didn't want to be rude either.

"Your mother seems very nice. Your father is a bit... distant. There's something harsh about him."

"He's ashamed of me, but ashamed of himself for feeling that way. He'd never admit it out loud but it's there."

"What did you do?" she asked turning back to him with concern creasing her brow.

"I was born like this," he spread his wings and arms, gesturing to his physical abnormalities.

Her concern flashed to confusion. "I don't understand."

"I don't look like the rest of the gods here. None of them have wings, few have tails and none are my color."

She looked him up and down before closing her eyes, brow furrowed with determination. She opened her eyes again and now there were grey pupils at their center. She squinted at him giving him a thorough once over. "I cannot see anything wrong with you. Wings are a gift, not a curse. I don't understand."

Armon watched her as she tried to figure out his family. "What about you? The sachee that raised you, were they kind?"

Her features went from puzzled to stoic as she turned to look out the window. "I look forward to living here. Among my own people. Where I'm not feared."

Armon felt a pang in his chest and had a sudden urge to pull her to him and just hold her. He knew all too well the pain of being feared by those around him.

"The gods here, they fear me," he told her more as a warning not to get her hopes up than an effort to gain her pity. "Don't be surprised if they find your power as unsettling."

"But I'll have you, and your mother," she turned to him as a smile spread across her face. "That is more than I ever had growing up."

"Then you--you want to be married? To me?"

"I'd like to get to know you first," she admitted. "But I believe so. Yes."

◆

Armon woke the next morning in his bed in Taivas. He threw his arms over his head and arched his back. He'd forgotten how nice it was to sleep in a real bed. Dragons slept on the ground and so did he usually. Occasionally he'd spend the night in the trees but only if it was raining.

A smile spread across his lips as an idea entered his mind.

Thirty minutes later he was washed and dressed and standing outside Dematri's door. He stared at the grains in the wood. He needed to knock. *Just make a fist, knock on the door and ask her if she wants to go see the dragons. No big deal. Just do it.*

He stood there another minute before taking a deep breath, forming a fist and lifting it.

Just as he was about to knock the door flew open.

"Oh, sorry, I thought you'd lost your nerve and gone," Dematri said with a smile.

Armon let out a nervous laugh. "Was it obvious?"

"I could see your shadow under the door," she admitted. "What did you want to ask me?"

"I just wanted to say good morning."

"You could have met me at breakfast to do that," she pointed out.

They stood in awkward silence for a
moment as he tried to figure out what to say to
her. She wasn't going to make this easy.

"I was wondering, if you'd come with me.
There is something I'd like to show you."

"Where are we going?"

"It's a surprise." He offered her his hand.
She slid her hand into his and he brought them
to the forest, just around the bend from the
dragon's keep.

"Where are we?" she asked. "Is that.... Are
there dragons?"

He smiled at the excitement in her voice.
He led her toward the nesting grounds with a
smile. Most of the dragons were off hunting
but a few had stayed behind to look after the
young. They looked at the couple but quickly
went back about their business. The little ones
raced over to Armon, spitting fire and ice in
their excitement.

"Oh my word!" she gasped. She knelt down
to let the first dragonling sniff her hand. The
young female rubbed her head on Dematri's
hand. "Armon!"

"The mother is the most beautiful creature
you'll ever see." He felt his smile spread.

"Where is she?" she asked looking around.

"She's likely hunting for fish in the ocean," Armon said. A large male approached them. "This is their father."

Dematri craned her neck to look up at him. "He's enormous!"

"He is on the large side." He reached up to scratch the dragon just behind the wing. "He's a gentle giant, though. At least, as far as dragons go. He'll still rip your head off if you threaten his young or his home."

"That's comforting," she laughed.

Just then, the mother dragon and the rest of the hunting party landed in the center of the clearing.

"Dem," Armon said touching her shoulder. "We need to step back as they eat."

She stood as the dragons all ran to the carcasses. The sickly sweet smell of blood filled the air as they began ripping the kill apart. The mother dragon tossed scrapes to her young. Her red and orange scales shown like fire in the early morning sun and her sea green eyes locked with his for a moment until her gaze fell to the woman beside him. She nodded to the pair before returning to her meal.

◆

"That was the most incredible experience of my entire life." Dematri beamed as they walked through the think undergrowth of the forest.

"I'm glad you liked it," Armon replied with a smile. His thoughts drifted to Nicitiva and her fear of the dragons. She had not appreciated it when he took her here.

"How much time do you spend down here?" It was an innocent question that caused the familiar swill to fill his stomach.

"More than I'd like to admit."

"What does that mean?"

Before he could answer there was a rustling in the foliage next to the path. Armon pushed Dematri behind him as a sachee stepped out onto the path to face them. His skin was a creamy orange with black swirled throughout. He wore the garb of a scout. A simple loincloth and a chest plate made of small bones. He had dragon teeth hanging from his left ear indicating he'd killed at least one of them in his life, a rite of passage when a boy becomes a man.

Dematri stepped out from behind Armon and gave him a quick glare before softening her gaze to address the man. "Hello."

He eyed Armon with rage before looking back to Dematri. "Hello, I wish to speak to the God of War."

Armon stepped forward. "Then speak to him."

"Come with me." The plea was enough to break Armon.

"Very well," he said before turning to Dematri. "I can meet you back in Taivas."

"I think I would rather tag along," Dematri insisted.

Armon gave a heavy sigh. If she was going to marry him, she should be by his side. "Very well."

The sachee warrior waited until Armon gave him a nod before turning and dashing into the forest. The gods ran after him deep into the forest until they reached a clearing at the edge of a lake. A small village. The houses were mud huts covered in animal pelts. There was a path through the under growth down to the lake where a few children played in the water under the watchful eye of their mother. Most of the women were cooking and watching children. A few sparred in a nearby sandpit. There were no men. Even the children were all female.

"Where are all the men?"

"Dead," he said, standing. "Excuse me for asking, but how do you not know that?"

"I'm the god of a large land mass with two cultures who pray to me." Armon felt like an ass making excuses. In reality, he'd been avoiding his duties.

"I'm sorry."

"Don't be. What's your name?"

"Redder," he answered. "What can I call you?"

"Armon, this is Dematri," he said. Women were gathering around and the children were hiding behind them.

Dematri smiled at them. Offering her hands they took them and began talking so quickly and quietly that Armon couldn't make out the words.

"I'm sorry," Armon said, looking around.

"What do you mean?"

He looked in the young man's eyes and couldn't face what he'd done. He'd let everyone down. He should have punished the ones who hurt the weak and brought victory to those trying to defend themselves. But he'd been too busy wishing he were someone else.

He couldn't find the words.

"Just know that I'm sorry."

Dematri took his hand. A gesture he recognized and an attempt to comfort him.

He shifted them to the other side of the lake.

They walked in silence for a long time. Armon knew he'd been neglecting his duties but he never considered what that meant for his people.

"How long has it been since you stopped listening to them?" Dematri's voice was soft and careful.

"Years." He'd been so wrapped up in his own self-pity he'd forgotten about them.

"When I came of age and starting hearing the prayers, it was difficult. Some of them are so petty. So needy, every little thing is the end of their world." She walked slowly forcing him to slow his pace and listen. "So I stopped listening."

He frowned. "For how long?"

"A few days. I suddenly felt this... this fear deep in my belly and I knew someone needed me. It was a young elven girl from Tama," she said with a smile. "She was lost in the forest and terrified that the sachee would find her and kill her. You know the Tama enslave sachee women and children so her fear was justified. Anyway, when I reached her, a smile broke across her face. I should have directed her mother to find her but honestly, in the moment, I needed to know I was needed. That I could make a difference in the world. And I did. I brought her home. I tucked her into bed that night. Her mother held my hand and thanked me over and over again."

"Why did you tell me this?" Armon asked feeling even worse about what he'd done.

"Because Armon," she said, taking his hand. "We all stop listening sometimes, the important thing, is to start again. You are needed, Armon. You are necessary."

"I left because, I interfered," he'd never told anyone this. And it scared him more than he cared to admit to tell her now.

"What do you mean? You answered a prayer?"

"A group of elves decided that it would be a good idea to make a sacrifice to me. They chose one sachee child and one elven child. Both from the street. Both orphans with no one in the world to care about them." He took a deep breath trying to calm himself but the rage threatened to over take him even years after the event itself.

"What did you do?"

"I was so angry, I just reacted. I killed them," he paused. "I ripped them apart. But I was so wrapped up in my rage over the deed, I didn't notice the children were watching. They saw everything. And when I turned to them, when it was over, they screamed for help. Even louder than their cries had been when they faced death. I'm a monster Dematri, I have no place in this world."

◆

Armon felt himself getting caught up in all that was Dematri. She was his equal in every way. He didn't have to hide who or what from her. She had a childlike innocence about her that was so freeing. He didn't think of Nicitiva very often any more. Occasionally he'd feel a pang of guilt for not going back to her, but she was a queen and he was a god. They could never be together and the sooner she knew that much of the truth, the better.

He stared at the waterfall in the garden and the fish circling the pond below. He needed to tell her he wouldn't be seeing her anymore. He owed her that. He might never have been open enough to accept Dematri if not for the time spent with Nicitiva. Just as he was about to go to her, a soft hand slid over his bare back.

He turned to see Dematri. Her smile erased all thoughts of his former lover.

"Good morning," he said. He wanted to lean in and kiss her but a small part of him feared she'd recoil from his touch.

As if she could read his mind, she stood up on her tiptoes and placed a quick kiss on his lips.

Armon felt something strange in his chest. An overwhelming feeling. It was like his chest was full, he could barely breathe and something tugged the corners of his lips up into a crooked grin. "Let's get out of here."

"Where should we go?" she asked.

"Let's go check out the city, I want to show you my favorite place." He offered her his hand.

"I've never been in an elven city before." Dematri looked nervous.

He felt a laugh bubble up in his throat. "You'll like it, I promise."

"I suppose." She took his hand and they were in a back alley of Taliz. he led her toward the ocean.

Armon sensed the uncertainty in her and looked over his shoulder at her. "What?"

"Sachee and elves don't exactly get along. I've never interacted with elves before."

"You'll do fine, I'll do the talking if you like. And you can jump in whenever you're ready." He paused. "Can you change your appearance? To match the elves? The experience is much better if they don't know what we are."

She gave a shrug and her white hair turned blond and her skin darkened slightly. Her eyes grew electric blue irises, but no pupils. Armon smiled. She was unique, even when she was trying to blend in.

He changed his own appearance and offered his hand once more. She took it and he lead her into the belly of the city.

Dematri stared at the market in awe. Armon placed a finger on her temple and let her see it through his eyes.

"Everything is so dull this way, how do you stand it?"

Armon laughed as he took in the vibrant colors glittering throughout the market. "Not many would scoff at such a gift."

"It's not my fault my vision is more stimulating than yours." She placed her hand on his temple and the dull greens, reds, and browns of the market were replaced by bright blues, oranges, and yellows, with deeper blues and greens in the shadows.

"Brighter, but it lacks definition. How do you not stumble as you walk?"

"I walk slowly. And generally have no issues."

"I suppose I shall keep my eyes and you should keep yours then."

"I think that would be for the best. I might get depressed if I look through yours for too long."

"And I may start having fits."

The market was busy; Armon watched excitement flutter in Dematri's eyes as she looked about the tents and stalls.

The sweet smell of the baker's honey rolls floated through the air invading their senses. Dematri's belly rumbled.

"What is that?" she asked.

"Would you like some?" Armon asked gesturing to a stand with a plump woman holding a tray of rolls that were covered in sticky honey and nuts. She nodded.

"Go find us a table, I'll buy some."

"Table?"

He placed both hands on her shoulders and turned her to see a patio overlooking the bay and all the ships. It was covered in tables and chairs. Complete with sea birds picking at left over and spilled food. She wandered over and found a table before he turned back to his task.

Once he had the bread, he returned to the patio. The birds took notice of her. One pecked gently at her skirts as he approached. The bird flew away in a hurry at the sight of him. Being the god of war and chaos wouldn't win him any medals or any bird friends apparently.

"I snagged these as they came out of the oven," he beamed. She picked at her roll and looked out over the ocean.

"This is very good," she said with a smile. "We didn't have anything like this where I grew up."

"What was it like?" he asked. "Growing up with...," He refrained from using the term sachee, the patio was crowded and the sachee were not exactly a good topic in present company.

"It was cold. Not physically. Emotionally." She didn't look at him as she spoke and her tone became distant. "They made sure I was well fed and otherwise taken care of, but they knew what I was. What I am. So they were afraid of me. I had no friends. Except the young ones. They hadn't been taught to fear me yet." A smile spread across her face. "They were my only joy. But each one would eventually understand what I was and stop coming to see me. Even if they didn't want to, their parents made them. And I was forgotten."

"Forgotten?"

"Once I was old enough they put me on the mountain top. They were afraid I would do something. I have no idea really. But I was alone. Until your mother came to get me."

Armon contemplated what she'd revealed to him. She needed him. She needed to belong somewhere. And she needed him to see that. What she didn't seem to realize was that he needed her too.

His mind full and his stomach uneasy, he abandoned his bread to look into the market. Maybe marrying her was the right thing. Maybe she did want to be his wife. His mind wandered to Nicitiva. She made him feel wanted. But she'd never really seen him. Dematri had. And still she looked at him with kindness and understanding.

His gaze fell on a woman in a copper colored gown with long flowing hair. A smile spread across his face as he recognized Nicitiva. As quickly as it had spread, it faded. She turned to face a vendor and her swollen belly was unmistakable. What were the chances she'd let her husband warm her bed when Armon had stopped showing up?

◆

Armon brought Dematri back to the God's Realm, Taivas, and showed her to his mother's gardens. As she explored he tried to figure out how long he'd been absent from the elven kingdom. Time moved differently here, but he doubted it moved fast enough to absolve him of this particular deed. He should have been more careful. He'd never heard of a god impregnating an elf before. He'd just assumed it wasn't possible. He fought the rage in his chest and the urge to lash out. How could he have been so stupid?

"Dem," he said gently, taking her hand. "I need to go take care of a few things. Would you like me to find my mother for you before I go?"

"I think I can manage on my own. But I want to show you something when you return." There was a gleam in her eye and happiness about her features that managed to lighten the weight, he'd thought to be permanent, on his chest. She was something special. He was lucky to have her.

He turned around and was in a back alley of Taliz. He changed his appearance and moved to search out Nicitiva. It was late in the day and the last of Ma Bet's suns set over the ocean, painting the sky brilliant reds, oranges, and pinks.

Taking a deep breath to quell the upset that rose in his stomach, Armon took a moment to observe the view from the palace steps. The kingdom sprawled before him, tinted pink by the setting sun. The shadows were a deep purple and few elves were about.

Still uneasy, but determined, he turned and entered through the servants quarters. A few men tried to stop to talk to him but he waved them off. He needed to find out the truth. He needed to know if the child inside Nicitiva was his.

The stairs leading to her chambers seemed steeper than he remembered. By the time he reached the top the sun had settled beyond the ocean and the sky was dark purple. He placed a hand on the door and listened. Faint humming drifted from inside. It was the same old fisherman's tune she favored.

He pushed away from the door. Maybe he should just leave her alone. He'd done enough damage. He needed to be in Taivas with his people.

Just as he was about to leave the door swung open. Nicitiva's eye grew with surprise and a smile spread across her face.

"Bahn!" she shouted. "Where have you been? I have great news!"

"I can see that," he said with a smile that didn't quite reach his eyes.

"It's yours." The pride in her eyes took him aback as she placed two hands on her belly and swayed. "He's going to be king someday."

"Y-y-you're certain it's a boy?" Armon stammered, unsure of what he should say. She took his hand and placed it on her belly. The tiny creature inside moved against his palm. A smile spread across his face. His baby.

"I'm certain. The gods will bless us with a boy. And when we marry, you will be King."

Armon took a step back. "When we marry?"

"Of course." Her smile faded and anger pinched her eyes. "You don't think I would raise my child with that brute do you?"

"How do you propose we go about that?" Armon snapped anger bubbling up inside. At least, he told himself, it was anger, and not panic. Gods did not have children with worshipers. How could he let this happen? He held his hand, running his fingers over his palm and remembering what the child felt like moving against it. His child, his son. "I doubt he's going to step aside and let me take over. I have a life Nicitiva, I have responsibilities."

He sounded pathetic even to himself. If he'd known before meeting Dematri he might have done it. Might have lived as king and raised his child with her. But now, eternity didn't seem so dark or lonely. He didn't want to leave Dem. He hated being apart from her even now. But he couldn't abandon his child either.

"You have to kill him," Nicitiva said. "Obviously."

"I won't kill an elf without cause," Armon said. The conviction in his voice surprised him. He was the god of war and chaos, was he not? "If you want me to be with you for this child, you will just have to leave him."

"I cannot leave him," she shouted. "He would kill me!"

"I wouldn't make you do it on your own," he snapped. Of course, if he stayed he'd need to tell her the truth about himself. That wouldn't go over well and then she'd really be in trouble. "Look, don't do anything until I get back. I have things I need to take care of before anything else happens."

"It's not like I can hold it in, Bahn," she snapped. "The baby will come when he's ready and it won't be long."

He left without saying anything else. There was no point. She was furious, not that he blamed her, and he was defeated. This would change history. Even if no one ever knew the child's true parentage, he would be stronger, more powerful than the others. Elves would notice. Even his father, Dios, would notice.

◆

After several evening of unrest, Armon woke the to the sounds of a newborn infant. Its cries were distant but strong. Yeo must have delivered sometime in the night. The whole place would be all atwitter with well wishes, "oohs" and "ahhs." After a night of tossing and turning, he could only hope it would quiet soon.

His mind wandered to his own child. He would be here soon and then Armon would be forced to face Nicitiva, Dematri, and his mother and father. If he were smart he might have tried talking to them about it already. But every time he tried to broach the subject, he couldn't get the words past the lump in his throat.

He walked over to the washbasin in the corner and splashed water on his face. He looked at himself in the broken remnants of the mirror. His black scaly skin glistened with the droplets and his eyes seemed to burn in the dim morning light. Would it look like him? He'd changed his appearance to create the child maybe it would be born with his elven visage. Maybe.

The baby continued to wail and he felt a pang in his heart. Why wasn't its mother comforting it?

A subtle knock sounded at the door and he moved to open it without another thought. Dematri rushed in before he could even register who was there. He hadn't seen her since before he confronted Nicitiva. He didn't want her to see him. She'd know something was wrong.

"I know you're avoiding me!" she scolded pointing one accusing finger at him. "But you need to hear me out! I really like you, Armon. We had so much fun together, until you saw that elf. Which does worry me a bit, but she's an elf. Do you really want her more than me? I need to know so I can run away and hide. Possibly never be seen again." She gave a nervous chuckle and rung her hands.

"Dem." Sure he hadn't really explained himself but she couldn't think he didn't want her. Could she? "Of course I want you. But I'm no good Dematri. You deserve so much more. You deserve someone who does not run from responsibility. Someone who hasn't let down their people or made the mistakes I have."

The baby wailed even louder, pulling his attention from the woman before him. She placed a hand on either side of his face and pulled his gaze back to her glazed white eyes.

"Armon, you are all I want in this world. You make me feel normal."

Armon's heart soared at her words. But the smile was wiped from his face as the baby's cries turned desperate, painful.

"Why won't anyone see to that baby?" he snapped.

Dematri frowned. "What baby?"

"Can you not hear it? Its cries are so loud I can hardly think!"

"I don't hear anything Armon, are you sure it's a baby?"

Understanding hit him with enough force to knock the wind from his lungs.

"It's *my* baby."

Before she could respond he was in the Flacari palace, just outside the Queen's chambers. There were guards posted at the door but he didn't let them see him. He stepped through and found a cradle in the middle of the room.

No candles were lit and only a slim beam of sunlight slipped into the room from between the curtains. The cradle had white dressings but there was something strange about it. He stared but he couldn't figure out why they were so dirty. They were covered in splattered stains. He took several slow steps, despite his heart urging him to run to the child. Something wasn't right.

The handle of the dagger was ornate, inlaid with blue stones from the ocean. He knew it well. Though, when he'd purchased it, he hadn't thought it would be used to stab his child. The baby cried and the dagger wiggled with its movements. Armon's heart broke as he stared at his son. The boy had the same black scales as his father and a long, thrashing tail. They thought he was deformed, no doubt.

Armon placed a hand gently on the dagger and it vanished from the baby's tiny chest. The baby calmed slightly.

"You're safe now." Armon placed one hand on the child's head and another on his chest using his powers to seal the wound. The baby settled a bit more, still not completely satisfied with his care. Armon had seen people hold babies before, but he'd never tried it. Mostly because they would scream as soon as they caught sight of him.

This child opened its tiny red eyes to reveal they, too, matched his father's. He studied the man leaning over his crib. He was so alert for a newborn.

"It's nearly dead," the male voice from the other side of the door filled Armon with rage.

"You should have cut off its head, it's an abomination!" Nicitiva's voice was harsh but unmistakable. Armon changed his appearance before the door opened. He didn't look at them, knowing the rage in his soul would shine bright red in his eyes no matter how much he tried to conceal it.

"What are you?" she shrieked, moving toward him as she and the King entered. "What did you put in my womb?"

Armon stared at his baby. His beautiful little boy. Her hatred of the baby was so similar to his hatred of himself and yet, he could not forgive her. Not for this.

He turned to face her and let his elven appearance melt away. She took a step back and gasped. Her husband's eyes grew in fear.

"I am Armon." The calm in his voice surprised even himself. But he didn't want to scare the baby. He never wanted this child to fear him. "God of War and Chaos. *You* tried to kill my son and for that, you will suffer."

He extended his hand and the dagger appeared.

"No please, I didn't know!"

"You are a mother and he is your child, that is all you needed to know." Before he could plunge the dagger into her heart Dematri appeared beside him.

"Armon, stop!" He froze as she looked about the room and put the pieces together. "Your baby." she said looking into the crib. She looked to Nicitiva with a frown.

"She buried this dagger in his chest and left him to die," he growled. Dematri's eyes turned from white to black. She looked at the baby then to the Queen and King. She scooped the child into her arms and held him close. Her face remained stoic as she bounced gently and the baby fell asleep. One tiny hand on her chest

"How could a mother do such to her own child?" she asked looking at Nicitiva.

"I thought— I thought it was sick. Deformed."

"It looks very much like the native people of this land," Dematri pointed out.

"I never slept with any sachee." She didn't bother to try and hide her disgust.

"That you knew of." Dematri placed a calming hand on Armon's forearm until he lowered the blade. Reluctantly. His tail thrashed wildly in protest. "The Gods you worship are more sachee than elf. We are also more forgiving than elves."

"Oh, thank you!" The King fell to his knees, clutching Dematri's gown.

Dematri ripped the fabric from the man's hands and hissed in anger. "You will be punished!" Dematri walked in circles about the room, looking at the baby. "For you and your wife, a curse of infertility. You've proven yourselves ill-suited to parenthood."

"But the royal line!" The King said, standing up.

"Will die with you," Armon hissed through clenched fangs.

"You have also forfeited your immortality. You will age and die over the next eighty to one hundred years, should sickness not take you sooner."

Nicitiva bowed her head and wept into her hands.

Armon wanted to kill them now. Wanted to feel their skulls crack in his palm for what they'd done to his son.

"Come Armon," Dematri said offering her hand. "Let's go home."

Armon took her hand allowing the dagger to fall to the floor with a clatter. Nicitiva looked at them through pain filled eyes just as they vanished.

Armon took the baby from Dematri as soon as they were back in his chambers. "You should have let me kill them."

"Armon, I have to maintain balance. I cannot let you just kill a ruler before his time. Taking away his immortality was damaging enough."

"We need to make sure this cannot happen again. I did not think I could procreate with an elf."

"Why would you think that?"

"I do not know any gods who have created a child with an elf."

"It has happened, that is why most gods stay here. They do not spend time with elven women." Dematri stepped toward the mirror, placing a hand on the frame. The image of her faded, replaced by one of a small child crying alone in an alley appeared. That changed to a neglected infant in a cradle. Its siblings were dirty with sunken cheeks and rags hanging off their thin limbs. They lacked even the energy for play. "Children are taken for granted down there. They are a burden to their parents."

"What are you thinking?" Armon asked taking an interest in what she was doing.

"Armon?" The male voice sent a wave of irritation though Armon as he turned to see his father and mother at the door.

"What is that?" The venom in his father's voice made him furious.

"Your grandson," he snarled as quietly as possible so as to not wake the baby.

"Why is he here?" Dios asked. "He's only a demi god. He will not survive here for long."

"He is strong," Armon protested. "He survived hours with a blade sticking out of his chest."

Deviyan stepped forward to see the child. "He's beautiful, how did he come to have a dagger in his chest?"

"His mother," Armon and Dematri said in unison.

"I wish he could stay, Armon, but he cannot." His mother's voice was tender yet unyielding.

Armon had guessed as much before they'd brought him here. Still, it was like his heart was being ripped in two at the mere thought of sending him back.

"They will kill him."

Dios placed a hand on the baby's cheek and his black scales turned to tawny smooth skin. His tail receded and his eyes became the deep blue of all newborn elves.

"I cannot keep his power concealed forever, but he will be safe until he can protect himself."

"Where can we put him?" Armon asked. "Who will take him? No one wants the children they have let alone one that isn't their blood."

"When did you become so cynical?" Deviyan asked. "There are those who will love this child as one of their own. You simply need to look." She waved a hand over the mirror and the unwanted and neglected children vanished. In their place was a couple mourning the loss of their infant son.

"How did he die?" Armon asked suspiciously.

"Illness. One his tiny body was not strong enough to overcome." She looked from the mirror to her son. "Let's go, sooner is best in cases like this."

"Will I ever see him again?" Armon asked. There was an oppressive weight on his chest and a strange stinging in his eyes.

"You can watch him grow up. You can visit him. But it would be best if he never knew who you really were." Dios' voice was tender. Kind, in a way Armon had never heard from his father. Before he could protest, they were outside a small farm. The couple had livestock and a beautiful plot of land. There were rolling fields and tree covered hills. A small pond was on the southern border just before the tree line, the surface rippling as fish fed. It would be a great place to grow up. And secluded enough that if he did exhibit godlike powers he wouldn't become the talk of the town.

Deviyan placed a hand on the door and waited. The male farmer opened it a moment later, his eyes puffy and red with sadness. He looked confused by the group of visitors.

"Hello," Deviyan gave him a smile meant to put him at ease but he seemed to grow more suspicious.

"You cannot be." As the man spoke his eyes grew.

"We are," Dios said. "And we have something to ask of you and your wife."

"We've just lost our child, surely it can wait."

"It cannot," Deviyan gestured to the child still cradled in Armon's arms.

"What is it?" the farmer's wife asked as she pushed passed him out the door. Her eyes bulged as she took in the gods before her. "Will you bring back my son?"

"We cannot disrupt the balance in such a manner," Dematri said, stepping forward. "But we have come in the hopes that this child could find a loving home with you."

They looked at the baby and Armon reluctantly stepped forward. The woman looked like she wanted to snatch the child from his arms, but refrained. Her arms were out stretched and when he nodded, she gently took the child and cradled him to her chest.

"He is only half elf," Dios said. "There may be challenges in raising him."

"I am his father," Armon said. "I do not want to leave him. I have no choice."

The woman's expression turned to sympathy as she placed a hand on his scaled forearm. "You have given us an incredible gift."

He placed a hand on the baby's head. "I know"

"This child cannot replace what we've lost." The farmer's head was shaking as he looked at the baby.

"Even another born of your wife's womb could not replace the one lost," Deviyan said. "But this child needs a loving home, and you have so much love to give."

Armon leaned down and kissed his son's forehead. "If you ever need anything, call upon me. I will be here instantly."

The woman smiled up at him and he felt a strange warmth in his chest. She looked at his child like Deviyan looked at him. This was the place for his baby.

Armon's heart still hurt as he and Dematri climbed to the top of the tallest mountain in Ma Bet. It was deep in the Mecusilik Forest that connected all six elven kingdoms, though the forest itself remained mostly a place for the Sachee.

"Why can we not shift to the top?" he asked. Having the ability to simply be wherever the mind wanted you to be came in handy at times like these.

"Because it's beautiful, because you just lost your son and need time to process, and because you cannot simply poof yourself to the top of a mountain and curse an entire race. You need to be certain. You need to know exactly what you are doing and why. Mistakes come at a high price when you are a god. And I have no intention of making a mistake."

He frowned. *Curse?*

The air thinned and the temperature dropped. Snow covered the path as they continued to walk. It took them a few days to reach the summit and Armon felt worse than ever. The view was hidden by a blanket of cloud cover about a hundred or so feet down.

"You drag me up here and there isn't even a view?"

"Shush." She stared at the expanse as if she could see each and every being before her. Dematri extended her arms and closed her eyes. She was silent for a long time and Armon wondered if he should leave her be. He was about to turn around and give her some space when her voice boomed across the sky and lightening flashed all around them.

"A god was born of an elven Queen. Instead of seeing the gift she had been given, she saw only a monster. She attempted to kill the child. This offense is so great that I can no longer stand by in silence. From this day forward, you will have only two children. One male and one female. You will not be able to conceive until you have found the partner *I* have selected for you. Once married, men will be impotent to any woman but their wives. There will be no more unwanted children. There will be no more suffering."

She lowered her arms and the gasps and outcries of the elves echoed around them. She took a deep breath with tears falling from her eyes.

"It was necessary. They grow too fast and had no regard for life beyond their own. It is too late for the adults, but perhaps the children will grow to be better."

Armon pulled her against his chest. She looked up at him and he captured her lips with his own. They stood there for a long while, listening to the cries of their people. He knew his child would change the world. He just never realized he'd do it before he was even a week old.

THE
TEMPEST

V. S. HOLMES

About V. S. Holmes

V. S. Holmes is a gender-queer science fiction and fantasy author. She has written the REFORGED series and the NEL BENTLY BOOKS. *Smoke and Rain*, the first book in her fantasy quartet, won New Apple Literary's Excellence in Independent Publishing Award in 2015. In addition, she has published short fiction in several anthologies.

When not writing, she works as a contract archaeologist doing Cultural Resource Management throughout the northeastern U.S.

She can be found at her website as well as on Facebook, Twitter, Goodreads, and Instagram.

www.vs-holmes.com

THE TEMPEST

The taste of the ocean was the same salt as Nubon's blood. The waves beat in the pulse at her wrist, her throat, her thighs. Battered wood bit into her clenched hand. *Thirteen years and three days. I've heard the sounds of this sea for thirteen years and three days.* She absently wondered if the sounds of the womb she heard before were the same, an echo of this, much larger, water.

"It's almost dawn."

Nubon glanced at the man beside her. His sprawled stance lacked its usual playfulness. "Are you excited, *urhun?*" She had uttered the Berrin title for teacher a thousand times more than that for "father," and it held the same tenderness.

"No. Not today." His voice was as wave-beaten as the city bobbing at the horizon.

She heard Berinnal's streets from here, smelled the tar and kelp that kept the city afloat. The ships bearing the seven other potentials for the throne were visible, dark blots appearing occasionally through the morning fog. Nubon mentally ticked off her list. *Tua from the east. Buen from the south-east. Lebon from the south....* She continued, the words familiar in her mind, a touchstone she worried when her mind stormed. The snap of the junk's rigging dragged her eyes to the mast. The plain, dusky-orchid flag rose, the color of a warning sky. *And Nubon, from the north-east.*

A skiff slapped into the water. She followed Urhun down the ladder. This would be the last time they took to the sea together, at least, with her as his pupil. He pushed off from the ship, allowing her to simply be the passenger for the first time since they departed Berinnal a year ago.

"I think I'll miss this." She watched the knots of wrinkles in his beige face soften.

"I know I will." He paused in his rowing and looked at her as if her features were a map he needed to memorize. "Nubon Northeast. Remember everything."

"You taught me all I needed, I'm sure. I'll remember, I promise."

"You'll have to." Something darker shadowed the sadness in his voice. They could not speak about the week to come, the trials that would decide which of the eight scions could bear the weight of the Warlord's title.

Nubon forced herself to sit straight. Her tarred wooden armor was suddenly cloying. They were close enough to hear the smack of the others' oars. Close enough to see their faces were as apprehensive as hers. By the end of the day they would be enemies. Nubon looked to the city, glimmering like the inside of a shell in the sunrise. She wondered, for the first time in thirteen years and three days, what happened to the scions who failed.

◆

Flags rose from the tops of the eight towers encircling the wheel of the city. Crimson in the east, gold in the south, indigo in the west, violet in the north. Nubon's eyes traced the colors, like an artist's changing palette, until they rested on her own pink pennant. The city was still, the bustle she heard before dimmed as the soldiers ushered the cityfolk inside. No part of the ceremony would be betrayed by overeager shouts or pointed looks. The weight of their gazes through the salt-stained windows thudded into place over her armor. The skiff thunked against the leather-padded pilings, Urhun steadying the craft and looping its mooring around the cleat. Nubon swallowed her nerves with a gulp and hauled herself onto the docks. The collective awareness of the city swiveled from the horizon to the tanned faces of the scions.

The walk through the deserted streets was veiled, time passing as it did in dreams, glacial and all at once. Now leather and cooking fish overlaid the constant scent of salt and wood and tar. The city creaked with a large swell, the boards of the street muttering their commentary of the passing children. The hub of the city opened before her and she stopped. Apprehension ignited in her limbs, chasing adrenaline to her pounding heart. The others stood at the heads of the other streets. The changshan under their armor matched the nervous flags that announced their arrival. Nubon barely recognized the faces among which she had been raised. The fawn of their skin had weathered to tawny after a year at sea.

Friendships crafted from years of learning together were strained, uncertain. Drums rumbled through the central tower of Burme's temple, and Nubon's gaze flicked to the figure standing between the stilts of the open first floor. The Warlord's armor gleamed, every dent and scratch illuminated with gold paint. *This Warlord came from the south, then,* Nubon realized.

"You are here today to put to use all you have learned in the past year, and the twelve that came before them. You will be tested against one another, against the elements and the waves of Burme will decide who will take my place as Warlord of our people. You will survive only if you have a swift mind, a strong body, and a steady heart."

Urhun appeared at Nubon's elbow and she saw the others' teachers had arrived during the speech. He pressed a leather bowl into her hands, palm holding the cloth covering it in place.

The Warlord's hands raised.

"I am a drop in the sea, a thread in the fog," the scions intoned, "I am but a single wave in Burme's ocean."

Urhun tugged the cloth free of the bowl and splashed some liquid over the lump in the bottom. Smoke billowed from the bowl. Nubon gagged at the noxious smell. Urhun's hand clamped over hers, the other gripping the back of her armored neck. Only now did she realize the cowl of his jacket covered his nose and mouth. Her nose stung, lungs aching with each choking gasp. The city spun, the boards pitching under her feet as if the sea turned against them. The southwest scion across from her wobbled and fell. The buildings fell away. Nubon stared at the pulsing grey of the sky until darkness swallowed her.

◆

Smacking water. Bitter cold. Dragging weight. Nubon's eyes flew open. Air and water rushed into her throat with her gasp. She coughed, retching seawater. Her arms automatically swept through the water, legs pumping. Only when her lungs were clear and her body settled into the rhythm of treading water did she scan the horizon. The sun hung above the water by four hand-spans. Sleep fouled her mouth.

Is it mid-morning or mid-afternoon? She shook away the concern. Water already weighed her clothing. Her tarred armor was loose around her cold-shrunk body. She yanked at it, numb fingertips fumbling against the leather ties. Even in the height of summer the sea was deadly within an hour. Wet, dragging clothes would only hasten hypothermia. Every few minutes she glanced up, checking the unchanging horizon.

Her movements grew frantic as she struggled against the ties of her pauldrons. Seawater tightened the leather. Finally she yanked it free and turned to work on the next. She tethered each piece to the first, one tie clamped between her teeth to keep it from drifting. Finally she dragged the leaden changshan over her head. She cursed softly when it tangled in her braid. The more careful her movements, the safer she would be. Seawater made the dusky cloth the pink of angry flesh. She wrung the worst of the water from the garment and bundled onto her breastplate. Gooseflesh bloomed on her naked body. Breath billowed, inhalations mimicking the sweep of her arms, heart pounding with her churning legs.

The scales of the lamellar pauldrons and tassets moved like fish's skin with each swell.

"You will survive only if you have a swift mind...." Nubon forced herself to focus on the ordered scroll room of her mind. *Get out of the water. Find your bearings.* The first steps were key to survival. The horizon was barren. No land marred the smooth line. No smudge of birds betrayed a kelp-bed or flotsam. She checked the sun again. Three hand spans and a half. Thirty minutes had passed and it was afternoon. Nubon's broad mouth pinched closed. Perhaps it was the same day as her arrival, perhaps the next. She forced Urhun's face from her mind, shoved the seed of betrayal deeper into the twitching walls of her heart. She had another quarter of an hour before her muscles began to seize and the center of her body grew cold. *Fifteen minutes to find land.* Armor undulated, the light glinting dully off the smooth tarred surface. Her black eyes narrowed and she flipped her backplate over so it floated on the convex side. Her breast plate was next. She refastened the thongs she had just struggled to untie, tethering the shoulders together. The pauldrons and tassets she fixed to the sides. The interior was smoothed with leather, the exterior sealed and strengthened with tar and lacquer. Nubon was Berrin, and

Berrin children cut their teeth on shipbuilding. *Tar, wood, and cloth. The bones of a ship held together with faith.* She steadied the bobbing armor, hands planted wide, fingers splayed. She thrust herself up with the next swell and rolled onto her pitiful raft. Her thighs ached. Repetitive motion and cold froze her shoulders. All she wanted was to curl up on the warming leather and sleep. *Find your bearings.* She turned to the sun. They could have tossed her out anywhere. There was no way to tell where the city lay in relation to her, whether she should head east or west. The smallest miscalculation now would become miles in a few days. *Nubon Northeast. Remember everything.* Every lesson, every moment had been significant, a single pebble paving each scion's path to this moment. Her first lessons had been that everything could teach her something. Nothing was insignificant. She rose on her knees, weight spread between her bony knees on the breastplate and the balls of her flexed feet resting on the pauldrons. *It's been in my name all along. They tossed us overboard in the directions we were named after.* Her hands formed the blade of a paddle, and she turned her raft until she faced southwest. She expected a written test, like all the others in years before. Perhaps a practical examination of their weapon mastery and seamanship. She never imagined an actual trial against Burme himself. "Well?" She addressed the clotted clouds that were the ocean god's frown. Her hands opened with a comic flourish. "What do you think? I survived an hour." Hysterical laughter bubbled in her dry throat. The sound hissed through her teeth and died in the waves.

◆

Nubon rolled her shoulders, wondering through the cloud of sleep why her body ached. Her hand slipped from her bed and met with sudden, cold wetness. She surged upright. Her raft pitched to the left. She hastily spread her weight, waiting for the lurching armor to calm before moving again. Her chest burned with yesterday's movement of pulling her makeshift craft through the waves.

The sky was colorless in the east, a clear day's dawn encroaching on the night. Her tongue clung to the roof of her mouth, her teeth filmy. Her bladder ached with the need to relieve herself, but she balked at the waste of precious water. Air eddied about her bare shoulders and she shivered. *Wind.* Paddling was fine, but Burme's morning exhalation warned her to prepare for a blustering day. Her changshan was wadded between her knees, still damp and foul from salt and sweat. Her heart fluttered between her half-formed breasts and a steady throb built between her eyes. *Sail first. Then water.* She unrolled the mess of her former uniform, picking at the seams. She wished for her sailor's kit of knives, picks, and mending threads. They were forbade from bringing anything with them to meet the Warlord. She had not questioned the rule before. Her water-softened nail caught in the cloth. She yelped, sucking at the blood that welled from the torn bed. The nail hung, attached at one edge with pink threads of connective tissue. She eyed the fabric. "I should have worn hair pins." She needed a needle, something to cut the seams and poke holes large enough to stitch through. "And what should I sew with?" The words were hard, but not yet petulant.

Her gaze fell to the ragged nail. She tucked her shaking fingers against her lips, clamping the nail between her teeth. The thought spun her head and churned in her stomach. *It won't do any good hanging. It'll take a week to heal even if I don't rip it again. Make it useful.* She counted in her head, yanking her hand away on two, as if she could trick herself. Blood bubbled from her finger, running thickly down the side, pooling in her palm before continuing down her arm. She cradled her arm, cupping her hand to catch as much as possible while she rested the nail in the bowl of her backplate. She caught the blood on her tongue, tracing it back up her arm. She could not afford to bleed out here. Loss of water was bad, but the predators blood attracted were worse. She wedged her injured finger into a wad of cloth. She had bitten her nails most of her childhood, and it only took a second to nibble serrations into the long edge of the loose fingernail. She gripped it carefully and held the seam of the changshan taught between her knees. Well over a minute of sawing yielded some frayed thread. She glanced at the sunrise. She had half an hour before the day began in earnest, the heat sending wind scuttling across the water. She yanked at the threads, her carefully crafted saw clenched between her molars for safekeeping. The cloth was loathe to part, the thread requiring several more minutes of sawing before the first inches of seam gave way. She would starve to death before she opened the garment. "Dammit!" Her dark eyes squeezed shut and she inhaled through her wide nose. She was not known for patience. She needed water, and paddling was not as effective as a sail, but it was better than nothing.

She spread the cloth under herself, shifting her weight with deliberation. Water tightened the leather thongs connecting the scales of her lamellar pauldrons, but she managed to slip her middle and index fingers through two of the straps. Her palms cupped the curve of the pauldrons easily, the armor enlarging her hands and providing webbing like a duck's foot. She crouched over her armor and shoved her hands through the water. Her raft was far from streamlined, but it began to bob awkwardly southwest. Her arms swung up and forward, the circular momentum thrusting her forward. Her body lowered further, the motion becoming easier as her shoulders loosened. The muscles in her back bunched, tendons grinding over bone as her arms worked, like a great cat bounding forward. Her lips cracked with her grin, but she licked the blood away and pushed on. Her body sang with the steady heat and pain of new movement. She paddled until her body wept, until her arms could bear no more. Then she paused and sawed at her sail. Raw flesh bunched inside her cheek where she kept the ragged nail. Noon brought the beginnings of a sunburn. Her arms trembled and her stomach twisted in rebellion against her diet of blood and ocean spray. She wondered how far the city was beyond the horizon. *Our ships travel twelve knots. Assuming they bundled us on board immediately, they'd have just over nine hours to deposit me and turn back in time to be over the horizon before I woke.* The math was rough, but if she was pessimistic, Berrinal was just over fourteen leagues away. Her speed was barely a third of a junk's. *Five days. Fewer if I only nap.* She forced her arms into motion again. Without water she would not last three.

◆

The larger blister on her shoulder popped. Nubon wiped the fluid off her skin with a snarl. She was tired of betrayal. First Urhun, then the Warlord. Now her body. Her hands were cramped into claws, the leather straps of her pauldrons gouged pink canyons into her fingers. Her thighs, too, were tight with disuse, cold, and dehydration. She mentally ticked off the hours.

It was dusk. Sunset was a languid affair in summer, the light easing from the sky like a lover leaving bed, trailing gold sheets after herself. A kelp forest lay half a day northwest of the capital, and Nubon hoped to reach it that day. Either her speed was less than she guessed or they dumped her further out than she realized. The forest would bring Burme's blessing in the form of food. The creatures drawn to the forest, too, would be a boon. Nubon needed fish bones to sew her sail, and the watery meat would help rehydrate her body. *I know what I should do. It could buy me a few days, even. Enough to make it home.* Her abused stomach roiled at the thought. Finally she put her precious cloth aside where it would stay dry and tugged off her loincloth. Her abdomen ached and it took a moment to relax. She hated to urinate on her armor, but the leather would retain the fluid. When she was done, she crouched, cupping her hands. She breathed through her mouth, ignoring the warmth as she tipped the liquid down her throat. It was salty, almost oceanic, and bitter.

Her mind balked, but her parched lips welcomed the drink, regardless of the source. She forced herself to swallow another three handfuls before sweeping the rest into the sea and wetting a corner of her sail to wipe the leather clean.

Nausea hit high on her stomach, but she tightened her lips and settled in to sleep. Rest would help her forget her discomfort, and she preferred to warm herself by paddling during the night. Still, despite her exhaustion, she could not sleep. Night was cold on the water; sweat and wind drawing heat from her skin. The tie at the end of her braid broke hours ago. The straight, black curtain of her hair blanketed her shoulders. She rolled carefully onto her back and tugged half her changshan over her bare chest. "I wonder if you're being kind to us," she confided in the ocean god. "We called this lake Burme's eye, we call the wind your breath. I've yet to face your fury, here, alone, without hull to protect me. Have you tested the others more harshly? Have they survived? Perished? Will I ever see Berrinal on the horizon again? With each test I pass, will you bring another, worse, obstacle?" She worried the chewed flesh inside her cheek, grateful the coppery taste erased the salt of urine from her tongue. Her body was too parched to bother with tears, but her chest heaved. The barely-quenched flesh of her throat popped with her dry sobs. *Or have I already failed?* She bit back her words, allowing them to rattle around her mind instead. Some thoughts were too private for even a god to hear.

◆

The sound of the waves changed. It was not the rhythmic *kissh* of the water on her makeshift gunwales, though that remained, softer. Irregular smacks interrupted wet rustling. Nubon slowed her paddling, ears straining through the night, dark eyes narrowed. She wished suddenly for the blue light of Oura's lantern, the moon.

Instead, velveteen blackness cupped her eyes, filled the whorls of her ears with muffled sound. The smack came again, echoed by another, this one softer. She drew a slow, testing breath in, first to her right, then her left. The ocean was bitter, the salt so familiar it could have been her own odor. Fetid sweetness lay under the water's tang. *Rot.* There were thousands of creatures on the water. It could have been a bird, a swordfish, floating belly to the sun while tiny silver mimics of itself nibbled the bones clean. *Or it could be another scion who failed Burme's trial.*

She forced the morbid thought aside and riffled through her mental scroll-room. The stars were clear, though a smudge of clouds threatened to obscure them more than once. The bright blue star at the tip of Numeon's Scepter almost dipped into the black water. There was an hour's wait before dawn bloomed in the east. *If it's an animal, I can eat it. If it's a scion they might have tools I don't.* When the next faint slap came, she eased herself south. The sound grew closer. Other noises joined it, made sinister in the darkness; water sucked loudly, gurgling. A shape loomed out of the dark, stretched and white and stinking. Victory exploded in her gut, igniting her hunger and burning away the despair crouched between her ribs. Whatever it was, it was big, and dead, and not anything resembling her peers.

Another swell smacked against its blubberous side. The creature rolled, exposing more of its white, bloated belly and a half-eaten fin. Nubon lunged, grabbing onto the fin and dragging her tiny craft closer. Dawn would allow her to explore the carcass more thoroughly, but now she shoved globs of greasy blubber into her mouth. Her fingers dug into the limb, probing for the fibrous muscle. The first pieces were tangy and slick with rot, but those deeper, still protected by the bulk of the animal, were sweet. It was tough, more sinew than meat, but she barely bothered to chew it before swallowing, her watering mouth defying her dehydration. Her shrunken stomach ached, but she ignored it, stuffing herself until the skin over her stomach was uncomfortably taught.

Nubon smiled at the pink dawn, despite the weather it foretold. She was tethered to the fin of a massive creature, a monster of the deeper sea. The swollen belly was mottled white and grey, mimicking the movement of sunlight through the ocean's surface. The carcasses of the great monsters usually sank to the bottom once they burst, but this one was caught on a reef. Its four limbs were broad and paddle-like. *Either a lio or a maus, then.* She took stock of the creature. She would need to gut underneath to see how much had been scavenged, but she wanted two of the ribs for gunwales on her raft, and one of the teeth to use as a knife. She shoved the carcass roughly, dislodging any smaller scavengers that might antagonize her. She then paddled carefully around the creature, scanning the clear depths for larger predators. Despite the abundance, anything nearby would fight fiercely over a feast this large.

She finally shored her raft up on the fin again. She plunged into the water. It was warm in the relative shallows of the reef and the water green. Several paces deeper, the bulbous reef rising from the coarse sand. The colors were brilliant, even through the lens of dawn light. She panted deeply, drawing as much air into her lungs before inhaling slowly and diving. The carcass was very different under the water. Flesh floated, blubberous lace drifting from the pink and grey ruins of the massive predator. The ribs were not as bare as she had hoped, but a wound in its side told her how it died. She swam to its head and began worrying at a tooth, rocking it too and fro in its socket. It was already loose from some other, older battle. It came away with a bloom of clotted purple blood. She turned carefully in a circle, checking for predators again before surfacing for air. She turned to a cloudy eye with her new tool, picking the connecting muscles and nerves away until she dragged the orb from its socket with a sickening sucking sound.

She devoted her second dive to her gunwales. The wound in the creature's side was chewed away, the gleaming white of a few ribs showing through. They were as big around as her arm, and half again as long as her own height. She raked the tooth along the rib's length, peeling flesh as she went until two white arcs gleamed through the mess of butchered flesh. She could see, through the bars across the windows to the thing's gut, the meal that had been its last. She stabbed the tooth into the joint between spine and rib, working the sharp tip through the knot of milky cartilage. She swam lower, gripping the loose ventral end of the rib and dragging it upwards until it snapped free. She thrust to the surface, bubbles streaming from her mouth. She laid the rib across the bulging gut of its former owner and went to work on the second.

Intestines trailed from the hole she opened now, purple, knotted ropes. Tiny fish pecked at her feet and legs, puzzling over this new addition to their feast. She pried the second rib loose, and it came away easier with its neighbor gone. She propped it next to the first. She embedded the tooth in its stomach for safekeeping before fastening the ties of her back- and breastplate to the ribs. Cartilage and fat still slicked the bone and her battered fingers slipped twice. Next she turned to her sail, popping holes along the sides of the now sleeveless changshan. She left one side seam intact and ripped the sleeves into strips. *Now for thread.* The hanks of fresh sinew from the creature's fin lay on her raft. She pressed the tooth into them, grinding the tissue between the point and the armor. The sinew remained unaffected, too rubbery for the massive tooth to be of much use. She growled, pounding her fist against the swollen carcass. She needed something with a fierce edge, a metal or stone knife. *Or bone.*

With the sail and rigging tucked into her breastplate, she dove into the water. A quick glance told her she was still alone. *Perhaps whatever killed this thing broke some bones in the process.* The meat fell away from the wound, showing splintered ribs and torn organs. Whatever had attacked it bore sharp teeth. *If only I can break off a sliver of that rib.* She reached deeper, her arms sunk into the cavity for leverage. She glanced behind her. The last thing she needed was a predator to find her up to her elbows in a body. A smudge appeared in the distance, blue against the bright green of the shallow water. A school of fish, perhaps, or something bigger. She pulled harder, fingers slipping over the fat-slick bone. The sharp edges bit into her fingers, slicing into the meat of her palm. Something moved in the darkness of the cavity. A face, moon pale, cradled in a bloom of black hair. The scion's eye sockets were raw, all but the bare bone nibbled away. Nubon shrieked, bubbles exploding from her mouth. "Tua!" The ocean swallowed the sound. The other girl's corpse was naked and ended at the pelvis. Her hands still gripped the driftwood spear she used to gut her attacker from within. Nubon thrust herself to the surface, stomach heaving. She retched, vomiting half of her gluttonous meal. A swell buffeted her shaking body. *Tua.* Nubon spat seawater and bile from her mouth and swam to her armor. She hauled her shuddering form out of the waves, guts still roiling in rebellion. She flopped onto her back, unable to control the shaking in her limbs despite the warm breeze. Something surfaced just to the north, a slick, brown body and bladed fin. Her fingers fumbled in their makeshift webbing, tugging at the fabric looped around the fin. The shadow moved under the carcass, undulating with unhurried threat. She noted the armored head, it's length almost twice that of the lio. She shoved off, pushing her hands through the water, hoping each paddle would not bring the predator below surging to the surface after her.

Rising wind mocked her unfinished sail, whipping the waves and rocking her new gunwales. Tears and spray stung her salt-burnt cheeks, searing red tracks down her face. The bullfish exploded to the surface behind her, jaws snapping closed around the carcass. Old blood and fat splattered Nubon's back and she shuddered, thinking of Tua, twice consumed by monsters. Her hands trembled. *How can this help us find our Warlord? All this tells us is whether we have luck on our side, whether Berme even still looks down upon us.* She swallowed a sob. *It's been generations since the gods took enough interest in us to show their favor, or their scorn, even.* Nubon's raft was tiny in the face of the ocean, the creatures under the surface, the overcast sky above. It was insignificant under Burme's empty gaze. Survival took too much energy for her to break.

Not now. Even with every breeze and creature in her favor, it would be days before she returned to Berinal. She blinked back the rest of her tears. She would not give Berme the victory of her tears. He all ready had enough of her.

◆

Jaws closed around her, gnashing teeth tearing at her limbs. Hot, wet blood dripped down her legs. The lio's carcass rose before her, more fetid and rotting. The ribs parted before her, Tua's bloated corpse drifting closer. Nubon did not see the girl's narrow chin and round cheeks, but her own oval face.

Nubon jolted awake, breath shrieking in her abused throat. Hunger burned high in her gut, and a deeper ache crouched between her hips. Her subconscious took stock of her belongings. Her sail pieces had not been lost overboard and the leather ties were still firm around the ribs. She sat up and warm, wetness pooled between her legs. Blood coated her thighs. "Another test?" Her voice cracked over her bitter words. She was not old enough for her bleeding to come at predictable times. Yesterday she dismissed the dull cramping as dehydration, or the need to urinate, or battered muscles. She fumbled around for the tooth. Her hands met nothing but fabric and battered leather. She groaned. In her fear and horror that morning she had dropped her precious tool. It now rested somewhere in the rough sand of the ocean's bottom. She needed to deal with her blood, and quickly. Her sail was too precious to use a piece, and without the tooth she would be hard-pressed to tear the cloth. In her vain searching for her weapon, her fingers stilled on the shoulder padding of her breastplate. The leather was soft there, stitched over a layer of sea sponge padding. Her hands scrabbled at the thick hide, opening nothing but the bed of her torn fingernail. The leather was fixed to the wood and tar with metal tacks. She bent forward and clamped her dog teeth on the lining. It was salty and the acrid taste of tar burned her tongue. She tugged, uprooting the tacks, metal screaming as she dragged them from the wood. Pain flooded her jaw. Her vision exploded in whiteness and blood filled her mouth. Sharp fragments of her upper dog tooth pricking her tongue. She spat and spat again. Her vision cleared, the pitching waves and bloody leather rising through the cloud of pain. The lining had come free, the corner loose enough for her to shove two fingers underneath and pry the sponge loose. The first piece she pushed inside herself, wincing at the scrape of her dry fingers. The second, smaller, chunk went into the raw socket of her tooth.

Pain throbbed through her jaw. Even if she found food, she would struggle to eat. Her foray on the carcass and subsequent exhaustion wasted precious time. That she had yet to find the kelp bed to the northeast of the city, told her she was wildly off course or slower than she hoped.

◆

Her heart thundered between her ribs, the dance of nerves and excitement. *Birds.* Birds meant land, or at least, enough fish to warrant the trip this far into the sea. She lifted her nose to the air and sniffed. The sweetness of blood and her own sweat. Salt, of course. Beneath that, the tang of her leather armor. And something else, a rich, heady scent, but so faint she would have wondered if it was her hope tricking her, a mirage of the heart.

She waited for the next eddy of wind and drew a second breath. The scent came from the south. She threw her shoulders into her paddling, every piece of her body awakening at the prospect of the kelp beds. Her stomach rumbled, her heart thundered with new vigor and vicious cramps faded to aches.

The flock of sea birds massed above the bed, seething and diving after the small fish gathered among the kelp. Something bobbed above the fronds, jetsom of some sort. *Probably from when they dumped all of us overboard.* Her bitterness had faded to contempt in the wake of bigger worries, but it still pierced through her focus occasionally.

"Ahoy!"

She straightened, wondering for a moment whether her companionship-starved brain was hearing words in the bird calls.

"Oi!" The second call was clearer and the lump floating on the kelp bed raised two thin and very human arms. "Nubon, is that you?"

She almost capsized in her effort to paddle closer. The figure was silhouetted against the afternoon sun, but she thought she recognized Toren North's shaggy hair. After another minute of frantic paddling she drew within arm's length of the other scion. He was bare, like she, save for a tidy bandage on his left calf. "How long have you been here? Did you find any of the others? Are you alright? What happened?"

He laughed at her barrage of questions, but fatigue ran deep in his eyes. "I've been here a few days, trying to get the strength to row further. I met Urnese yesterday I think, hard to tell, I've got a bad fever." He gestured to the leg.

"Did she go on without you?"

"No, she's diving. Hunting for mussels." He settled himself with a low groan. "I'm next to useless, save for when there are actual fish. She couldn't catch a fish if Burme himself came down as asked, but she can hold her breath longer than any porpoise."

Nubon grinned. "It's good to see another person." She had not realized how much she missed other people until her eyes lit on the familiar planes of Toren's face. After a year and a day out to sea, crowded onto a junk with a dozen sailors, solitude had worn on her in unexpected ways.

"You saw no one else?"

She looked away. Tua's mangled face appeared unbidden in her mind's eye. "No one still alive."

Toren paled. "Who?"

"Tua. A lio got her. She gave as good as she got, and without her I'd never have made it this far." She ran a hand down the ribs forming her gunwales. Her gaze fell to the makeshift raft Toren perched on. Like her, they had used their armor, but with the added layer of their changsang's wrapped over the top and drenched in what looked like grease.

The two pieces of fabric were bound together with rough stitches of what looked like hair. *Urnese's, then, she's the only one with hair longer than mine.* Toren shivered and she frowned. "What happened to your leg? Is that why you've a fever?"

"Reef eel. Diving for some spines to make a needle. They're mouths are filled with foul things, small wonder it's infected."

Nubon cursed herself silently. She had been so preoccupied with the lio she had not thought to salvage anything else from the reef it snagged on. "How many days have you been like this?"

"Four, it's a slow burning one, so I think I'll make it. The dreams have started though, and the chills don't do me any favors."

Urnese surfaced with a gasp, flipping her hair from her eyes. Relief chased exhaustion from her features for a moment at the sight of another person. She did not speak as she paddled to the rafts. Nubon helped haul the other girl onto the raft, grinning as Urnese spat out a few mussels.

"Good haul."

The taller girl shrugged and pulled more of the shellfish from a fold in her loincloth. "There are plenty down there, but I can only carry a few at a time."

Nubon let Urnese scan her body and craft before gesturing to the ribs and unfinsihed sail. "I've got the gunwales, you've got the sewing. Strap our rafts together and sail home?"

Urnese's reserved expression twisted. "You think we'll be allowed back in? They tossed us out here, most of us are dead. Those that aren't soon will be, I would bet my last bit."

Toren rolled his eyes, but the gesture lacked his usual playful wit. "For someone set on dying, you're doing an awful lot to assure we don't. If we don't pass the test, so be it, Urn, but there's no point in despairing until we let out our last breath." He offered a faint smile.

Nubon drew a breath. She was glad Toren had been the one to find Urnese. She did not have the patience to deal with that fatalistic attitude for an hour, let alone a few days. She could not help adding, "Leastwise, if you're going to despair, do it to yourself."

Urnese sighed. "I'm sorry. I've been so hungry, and tired."

"I know." Nubon gestured to the two rafts. "I can fix these up with Toren if you want to keep diving. Do you have the air?"

Urnese's answering smile was cocky, almost confident enough for them both to forget how bleak their futures might be. "Of course." She swung her legs over and with a mocking salute and deep breath, slipped under the waves.

Soft hissing interrupted Nubon's judgements of the other girl. She glanced over at Toren to see that the sound was laughter. "What is it?"

"You and Urnese never got along. I find it funny that of the three people of find each other out here, you were two of them."

"Well there's no place for her dark thoughts here."

"And what about your foul temper? I'm sick and she's tired. We both could use help, but not if you're going to curse us at every turn." He softened the words with a squeeze of her hand. "Let's get this raft built. We've enough things trying to kill us without our help."

◆

Raw mussels were tasteless, but soft enough for Nubon to chew even with her shattered tooth. Toren's thin fingers worked Urnese's hair through what was left of Nubon's changsang. Theirs were too heavy from the blubber smeared across the fabric to keep it waterproof. Nubon slurped another mussel down and returned to the lio's rib. While Urnese dove for food, she and Toren had unfastened one of the ribs and navigated the other raft alongside Nubon's. It was still unsteady, but larger and more secure than lashed-together armor. The greased changsang came over top. Nubon worked now to fix the rib back to the side of the raft.

Urnese napped in one corner, her feet tangled with Toren's. It was unconscious, comfort drawn from familiarity. A flash of jealousy burned through Nubon's chest. She had not fostered any close relationships with the other scions, certainly not ones beyond friendship. Now she both wished she could draw the same comfort, and was glad she did not have the added complexity.

Her cold hands fumbled with the leather ties, but finally secured the rib to the raft. "We'll wait for proper wind, then head home."

Toren smiled, not looking up from his task of braiding teathers for the sail. "I'll be glad of it, and some part of me, I think, glad to give up the responsibilities of Warlord."

Nubon frowned. "You don't know that, yet. The three of us will return, and perhaps others. Burme knows what trials they'll put before us."

Toren shook his head. "You'll compete, surely, but neither of us stand a chance. Without Urnese I'd have bled out or succumbed to fever by now. Without me, she would have fallen to despair, or starved before we reached anywhere shallow enough to dive."

"And without you two I'd never have a sail."

Toren snorted. "You're bleeding, you're injured, you've had nothing to eat but rotted blubber and you still traveled three times as far as we. You have most of a sail, and would have used kelp to finish it, whether you found us or not. I think it's clear who Burme smiles upon, at least among the three of us."

Cold grew in Nubon's gut, a sensation that had nothing to do with the chill of the approaching night, or the eddies of air promising wind. Up until that moment surviving had simply been about not dying. *Now it's about passing a trial. Ascending a throne.* She shook away the anticipation and confusion the thought brought, and instead lifted her nose to test the breeze. It smelled the same, but with a bite.

"It's autumn."

"Yes."

She frowned, scanning the horizon. "'With his breath, Burme brings the ice to test our rigging, the wind to test our sails, and before his breath comes his vanguard to test our bones.'"

"*Mettle upon Metal,* third chapter, ninety-eighth verse." Toren looked up, then. "What is it?

She did not look at him, her gaze tracing the choppy waves in the distance. *There's not enough wind for swells that size.* "Burme's vanguard--Umsalun." The thought of Umsalun, the massive blade-faced fish, twisted Nubon's stomach. Each winter brought them migrating to the shallow, warmer waters closer to the western part of the sea. They were fast and deadly, and on their tails would come bigger problems.

"We need to leave." Nubon rose to her knees. "Get her up."

Great swells became tangled knots of waves, thrashing fins tearing the water's surface as the school approached. And on their tails came the great fins of a dozen different predators. Nubon shook the sail open. Toren's eyes were wide, fixed on the horizon. His skin was paler, now, Nubon thought, though perhaps it was just the fading light. "Toren. Now."

The boy straightened, then, and shook Urnese awake. Her eyes were still red and dull. "What?"

Nubon bit back her sharp reply. "Umsalun, coming this way. We can't be here when they arrive. The waves will be too big, not to mention the bullfish and lio that come for the slaughter." The blood roared in her heart, adrenaline tingled down her exhausted limbs. "Berme tests us again."

Urnese heaved a sigh. Despite the sullen look in her eye, Nubon could see the very real despair building in the other girl's heart. "It doesn't matter, Nubon. We're dead out here."

"Not yet we aren't. And I don't intend to be." She tossed Toren one of the sail's tethers. "Tie it down. There's enough wind to pull us clear before the hunters get here." She did not wait to see if he obeyed. Her fingers looped the makeshift rope through the hook on Urnese's breastplate and tied it. Toren's weakened hands were slow, and she pulled it from his grip. "It's alright." She flashed a smile she did not feel and did the work for him. Urnese still sat, arms wrapped around her battered knees, staring at the oncoming chaos.

Frustration unfurled in Nubon's chest. *Toren has an excuse, he's probably dying.* She pointed to the final tether. "Do you mind, Urnese?"

The other girl's gaze tumbled to the rope, but she did not move.

Nubon's frayed patience broke. "I don't care that you think we're going to die! I don't intend to, so either move your arse or jump overboard. You'll do as much good being bait as you would sulking." The boat tipped as something large--larger than any swordfish--passed. She gripped the edge of their raft, one leg hooking around Toren's waist to keep him from tumbling over the side. Her free hand wrapped the rope. Another swell pitched them back and the sail caught. The rope snapped taught and she cursed. Now she'd never have the slack to tie, but there was no way her exhausted arms could hold the tether the entire way back to Berrinal.

"Alright."

"What?" Nubon turned, distracted, to look at Urnese. The boat rocked again, this time from the force of the other girl propelling herself into the seething water. "Oura's tit!" Nubon grabbed Toren's arm and yanked the boy towards the rope, wrapping it around his good ankle. "I'll be right back. Stay here."

"You leap in after her and you'll both be dead!" Embers burned high on his sickly cheeks. Fever glazed all but the deepest panic from his eyes.

"No time." She eased herself over the edge, forcing air from her lungs, and dropped. Even with the clear green of the kelp bed, Nubon could only see shadows darting between the twisting fronds, now impossibly tangled.

Even if a Umsalun did not impale her, or a lio's jaws shut over her body, like Tua's, the tangled kelp would drag her under. *There.* A glimpse of beige skin through the flashing blue and silver of the fish. Her lungs already muttered for air. She sank deeper and kicked off.

She read the buffeting water with the downy hair of her bare skin, as much as with her eyes. She followed the stream of bubbles down, deep into the dark. The dusk light barely reached through the tangled fronds and writhing bodies.

Urnese sank deeper as air streamed from her nose. Her pained expression was softened with the weight of water and impending peace.

Not yet, Urnese. You'll try my patience for many years, yet. Nubon fought closer, stopping twice to untangle her ankles. She caught the other girl's gaze.

Urnese's eyes widened and she shook her head, air exploding from her mouth. Her gaze slid to something over Nubon's shoulder.

Nubon dropped her legs and turned. The school was upon them, Umsalun darting between the fronds seeking food. Others, however, patrolled the edges, hunting for those that would challenge their territory. There, through the seething mass of black and silver: copper. Fishes did not bear copper flesh, not in this sea of iron grey and cold green. *Burme's vanguard.* She grabbed at Urnese's cold hand, tugging hard. With little air in her lungs, however, Urnese's weight dragged. Nubon snarled, bubbles frothing from between her teeth. Her chest ached. She did not have Urnese's diver's breath and wouldn't last much more than another minute.

Copper flashed again, brown in the shadows, crimson where the sunset ignited the slick skin. It was a swordfish, larger than any Nubon had ever seen.

It sliced through the kelp, navigating through the churning fishes as a ship through fog. And it aimed for them. She thrust Urnese away and up. Nubon had a second to brace herself before the creature collided with her. She twisted, the fish's blade slicing past the soft skin of her belly. One hand clenched around the flat bone. It was creamy ivory, slick with a thin layer of skin. She dragged herself closer, tucking her body against the Umsalun's as it whipped between the kelp fronds. Her legs wrapped around the creature's abdomen, feet locking just in front of the pectoral fins. One hand gripped the dorsal, fingers scrabbling for purchase on the rubbery sail. She wrested its head up forcing it to either turn in a tight circle or make for the surface. She could not afford to check to see if Urnese had come to her senses and made it to the raft. The fish spiraled, as if to scrape Nubon off with the cold hands of kelp. Her hand shot forward, joining the first on the creature's bill. The Umsalun burst from the waves.

Nubon was almost tossed away by the sudden weight of being above the water. She snarled air into her burning lungs. The surface spun below them for a second, for eternity. Compared to the churning and burbling of the sea, the air was silent. Her eyes fixed on the fist-size, red orb beside her head. She expected the creature's eye to be roving, mad. It was cold, calculated, and she swore it saw her very soul.

Her precious breath burst from her lungs as they slammed into the water again. Whatever terror rooted in her heart upon first seeing the monster was two-fold. Not the hot fear of panic, but the cold fear in the face of certainty. *Even the monsters fear the storm.* Strength flooded her limbs, exhaustion swept away in the tempest of her fury. She wrenched the beak to the side. Her feet slammed against the root of the blade. The edge bit at her hands, then a crack reverberated through the water. The fish writhed, beating hot blood and cool ocean water over Nubon. She blinked against the wash of black blood. The Umsalun thrashed several arm lengths away, clotted flesh and blood streaming behind it's broken skull. Nubon shot to the surface. Her legs burned from the effort after so many days of disuse.

"Nubon!" Toren's voice, hoarse and faint, arced over the waves.

She glanced at him, wincing at the stinging in her palms. Finally her gaze dropped to her hands. They were wrapped around the blade of the Umsalun's skull.

"Where's Urnese?"

Nubon shook the buzzing of victory from her head and stuck out toward the raft. She did not answer until Toren had helped haul her from the waves. She shivered under the sudden overcast sky.

"Nubon, where is she?"

"Gone." She could not bring herself to meet his eyes for a moment. "We were attacked by an--an Umsalun." She squeezed her eyes shut against the sudden wave of anger and guilt that churned through her gut. She drew a breath, then another, and raised her eyes to his. "Burme tested us, he sent a messenger. I tried to save her, but I could not save us both."

Toren reach out to the blade in her hand. His fingers stopped just short of the chipped edge. "And this?"

"The creature tried to kill us." She secured the last tether of the sail, finally, and turned south-west. "So I killed it instead."

◆

Nubon's chin dug a pink divot into her knees as she watched dawn approach. Her shoulders finally stopped their aching after two days without paddling. Toren curled beside her, sparse brows furrowed even in sleep. She glanced down at the boy curled beside her. Did he dream of Urnese? She both prayed he did and hoped he did not. Even now she could hear the thrashing of the waves, the fins of the mighty swordfish slicing through the water as they hunted fish. *And Urnese.*

Her dark eyes roved over the raft, checking tethers, ties, checking the sail. They finally rested on the pale line of the sword. *My sword, now.* It had broken part way down the shaft.

"She had a point, you know."

Nubon did not have to ask of whom he spoke. "And that was what?"

"Before you came, she said Burme had forsaken us."

"He was testing us."

"No. Not just the scions, Nubon. Berr. All of us. We devote our lives to him, to the other gods, but when was the last time they made themselves known? Truly? We tell tales of their fury, of Burme's blessing in the form of the schools of fishes, but they are all but shadows of what they once were. We tell of the great winds that carried our ships across the sea in hours not weeks. We prophesize of the coming of a great storm, a tempest that will bring us into greatness. But when was the last time any god showed their face when the priests invoked them."

Nubon shrugged. Toren was right. Urnese was right. The gods had been silent for years, generations even. *But if the gods are silent, then what was that creature? That was no ordinary Umsalun.* She straightened. "That's the definition of faith, isn't it?" When Toren's brow furrowed at her, she continued. "Trusting, even without proof? Burme may not have been invoked, the gods may be silent, but they're there. This creature I killed, this sword in my hand, that tells me they still watch us. The fish, the air, the waves, all of those things are the gods speaking, Toren. Perhaps they are just waiting for us to answer them in their own language." She straightened, her head tilting into the faint breeze. "There, you hear that?"

Toren raised his head. "What?"

"Creaking wood. Shouting." Her lips cracked as she grinned for the first time in a week. "Berrinal."

◆

The city had never looked so beautiful. Every flag waved, every tower and building brimmed with people. They had been sighted long before she and Toren noticed the sound of the city, she was sure. She strengthened her grip on the sail, dropping one leg into the water to act as rudder, steering them towards the bedecked dock. A gold canopy swayed above the crowd at the forefront of the docks. *The Warlord.* She nudged Toren. "Look like you're happy."

He snorted and offered her a weak smile. "I am happy. It's just a little tempered with hunger and...." He trailed off, swallowed hard, and turned his shadowed, fevered eyes to the city. "I just want this to be over."

For all the gathered people, and the gay decorations, the crowd was quiet, breath held until they could see the faces of the scions. Somewhere, she knew, the parents she had, once, that she did not remember, were out there. She wondered if they knew her. The thought drowned in joy when she glimpsed the face of Urhurn. One of the tattered fragments of her changsang was crumpled under her knees and she pulled it free. She shook it out, one hand still gripping the sail's teather. Her fist thrust to the sky, the pink flag catching the breeze. The silence exploded in cheers.

"Hear that, Toren? That's for us."

"That's for you, Nubon." His was voice quiet, but not bitter.

The raft knocked against the dock and Nubon caught a rope someone tossed down and moored them. A dozen strangers' hands reached down, hauled them from the ocean, finally. She did not know what came next. She did not care, only that it involve clothes and food and possibly a week of sleep. Her limbs shook, though whether from excitement or exhaustion, she did not know.

The city spun before her eyes and it was a moment before she realized it was due to Urhurn's embrace, rather than dizziness. She snaked her arms around his shoulders.

"I'm so sorry." She could not see his face, tucked against her shoulder, but she heard tears in his voice.

"It doesn't matter now." And it did not. "What now?"

"Toren will be tended. You too. Washed and dressed."

"Nubon Northeast."

Nubon pulled away, her head dropping in deference to the Warlord's low tone. "Yessir."

"Wash, dress, then you are called before our Assembly."

Her grin faded at the hard expression in his eyes. "Is something wrong, sir?"

"I should not have to answer that for you. You have half an hour."

She turned, searching for Toren's face in the crowd. His back was to her, and he limped toward the state buildings, one arm over his teacher's shoulder.

Urhun escorted her to a simple room, with the help of two guards. They did not meet her eyes, but she suspected they were not there for her protection. *Perhaps for my containment.* She did not know what she had done wrong, but the hard anger in her belly told her that she had, in fact, done something.

Urhurn rested a hand on her shoulder. "They'll bring you to the Assembly, but I'll be there too, in the crowd. Just get cleaned up. You'll feel better then. And you can't bring weapons before the Warlord, remember."

"Weapons?"

He pointed at her hand. She followed the gesture. Her fingers still gripped the Umsalun's sword. "Right." The door shut behind him and she was abruptly alone. After so many days of solitude, the sudden, overwhelming contact with others was so brief it seemed a dream. She set aside her blade and looked about the room. A tub of steaming sea water crouched in the corner. She stripped what was left of her bloody underclothes off and slid into the bath. It was hot enough to burn, but she did not care. Her skin flushed pink then red at the heat and her vigorous scrubbing. scratches and bruises were stark against her now clean body.

A fresh changsang and loincloth were folded on a bench. The former was plain, but bore a pink circle on the breast. *Do they make them for all the scions, not knowing which will survive, or do they hastily sew the patches when we arrive?* She fingered the tidy stitches for a moment. She did not know what would come next. She thought she would be heralded a hero, that she and Toren would be honored and they would choose between the two. *Unless another scion arrived first.* Her treatment thus far told her that was not the case. She felt more like a prisoner than a future liege.

There was no mirror, but she managed to tidy her hair and straighten herself. She had spent more time than necessary in the bath, and she expected the guards to return any moment. The sword glimmered in the corner, bloody and stark. She dipped it in the bath, rubbing the worst of the gore away before drying it. *No weapons.* She earned the sword, wrested it from Burme's vanguard with bare hands. It was a symbol of her struggle, of her victory, such that it was. *I'll be damned if leave it behind.* She slid it down the front of her shirt, tucking it against her under the plain belt.

When the guards returned, opening the door without a knock or greeting, she was settled on the bench, hands crossed before her and feet still against the wooden planks of the floor.

"Nubon Northeast, you are required before the Assembly." They were silent as they ushered her down a narrow corridor to the broad foyer before the Assembly hall. The murmur of the gathered crowd bloomed as the door opened and Nubon stepped in.

She did not crane her neck, but a cursory look told her Toren was not present. The room was dim, the light lancing in from behind the row of priests, and the Wavemasters and Warlord seated on the dais behind them. It was designed to hurt her eyes, make her feel exposed. *I spent a week naked on the ocean. Exposure no longer frightens me.* The head priest rapped a stick against the rail separating them from the crowd of gathered nobles and teachers. "Nubon, do you know why you are called before Burme and before this counsel?"

"No, sir."

"The trials are designed to find the scion most fit to be Warlord, to lead our people, to fight for our ways, the scion most fit to ride the waves Burme sends to us. You do understand that, do you not?"

"I do, sir."

"Please recount to us the manner in which you returned this morning."

"I have told you twice now, and you witnessed it with your own eyes. I do not see the purpose in telling you a third time." A week ago her voice would have trembled. Her hands would have shaken despite their grip on her changsang. Now her gaze was steady, her hands rested easily behind her back. "Might you tell me why we are here?" It was phrased as a question, but her words ended on a hard, low note that did not ask, but rather, demanded.

"We hold the trials so we might determine the one scion best for the honor and responsibility of Warlord. One scion. Not two. You returned to Berrinal with another child in tow. A Warlord does not afford themselves friends. This is the fate of our nation, Nubon Northeast. Not your nursery."

Cold settled between her shoulders, the aching kiss of too many days alone, too many days wondering whether she would live to see the next moonrise. She did not rescue Toren because she wanted a friend, because she needed support.

"You have been tested before this nation and before Burme and have failed. Relinquish your armor and weapon."

"You're wrong."

The counsel head surged to his feet, but the Warlord raised a hand. He leaned forward, settling his gold chansang around his knees. "Go on."

She felt Urhun's eyes boring into her, but did not look away from the Warlord. "'Know our strengths and when to use them.' Surely you recognize the line."

"I do. It is the fourth line of the Warlord's Oath."

"And the fifth line?" she prompted.

"'Even when they are not my own.'"

She gave him a crisp nod. "Yes, sir. 'Even when they are not my own.' Toren North is a fine fisherman. I am better at seamanship. Would you will your nation to starve simply because you, yourself, could not catch enough fish? Would you leave your warriors naked and defenseless because you, yourself, were not a tanner? I saved Toren not because I wanted companionship. I saved him because I would have been a fool not to. You claim I have failed before you, before Burme, but you are wrong. Burme tested me. He tested me with cold, he tested me with the wind. He tested me with the bullfish and lio that prowl his waters. He tested me with the death of my own, the unpredictable nature of my own flesh." She rose from her knees. "And now he tests me with you. And I promise, I have not failed. If you question it, you need look no further than this." She loosened the ties on her breast plate and drew the gleaming ivory blade from her shirt. "I fought Umsalun and I won." A moment passed and then another. The silence was thick on her tongue and heavy with the bitter tang of blood. She moved to the massive censer in the center of the altar before her and shoved the torch into the bed of scented coals. The smoke drifted sullenly for a moment then poured through the lattice.

She had memorized these steps before she knew the alphabet, committed these lines to memory before she tied her first knots. The priests were supposed to ask who came before them, but they stood, silent, jaws slack as she barreled on. "I come before you as Nubon Northeast, no longer a child of the Kahust

House." She ripped her armor free and it clattered on the hard floor. Blood dribbled from her reopened nail bed. "I come before you as Nubon Northeast, tested before Burme, tested against the might of the waves and the screaming wind." Her changsang was next. She worried she would be embarrassed, standing naked before the counsel and every head of House. Now, however, she raised her chin with pride. Her bare body showed the marks of her trial, the bruises and blood that strengthened her soul. The rack before her held the heavy armored collar of Warlord. Were this a normal coronation, were she not wresting the title from the clammy hands of the stubborn Wavemasters, she would now don the pink robes that denoted her last name. Instead, she lowered the leather and metal over her bare shoulders, fastening the clasps with steady, albeit numb, fingers.

"We do not recognize you," the Warlord intoned.

"If I had not passed, sir, do you not think I would be dead?" She met the Warlord's eyes and took a step up the dais and toward the altar on the Warlord's right. "Do you not think I would have perished in the gullet of the bullfish?" Another step. "Do you not think I would have succumbed to cold and starvation and thirst?" She was level with the man now. "Do you not think I would have been gored by Umsalun, Burme's very messenger?"

The Warlord rose from his seat and gestured to the altar. "If you are so certain, then finish the rites. Finish your oath. We will let Burme decide."

"You think I will fail because the gods have been silent." She lifted the ivory blade in her hand and dragged it lightly across her chest, over the thundering of her heart. Blood welled between her fingers when she pressed her palm over the wound. "I say: listen harder." She spread the blood across the upright copper disk followed by oil and the ashes of the incense. "By the ashes of your temples, the oil of your ocean, the blood of your people, I beg you hear this devoted warrior. I am Nubon Northeast, come before you to take up the responsibilities of Warlord." She watched the smear of blood and ash and oil trickle down the burnished metal.

"I swear by the salt of my blood

*I will follow the wind of your
breath
I will protect our people, from
the mightiest general to the
smallest babe
I will read the skies and waters
and face the storms
I will know our strengths and
when to use them
Even when they are not my own.
I will raise Berr upon my
shoulders as the swell buoys the
timber of our city."*

She bowed her head. *If I were wrong, I would be dead. My heart would be stilled within my ribs, no matter that the gods have been silent for a hundred years.* "I am Nubon Northeast. I am a drop in the ocean, a single thread of mist off the sea, a whisper in the storm."

The priest rose with a snarl. "We do not recognize you!"

Rumbling began, shaking salt from the rafters. The wood of the buildings groaned as if in a gale. Nubon's gaze flicked to the Warlord. His eyes were fixed to the altar. She looked up, rocking back on her heels. The copper disk buzzed on its stand. The oil and blood and ashes writhed. The face that took shape there was almost human, save for its perfection. It bore lines, as if the owner had weathered the ocean of millennia.

The Warlord knelt, though Nubon did not tear her eyes from that of the god. Fabric rustled, leather creaked as the gathered masses fell to their knees.

"Burme recognizes you." The voice rattled the metal of the disk, drew wining from the glass of the windows. "You are Warlord Nubon. You are not a thread of mist, not a whisper, not a drop. You are a tempest and the world will quake in the might of your fury." The torches exploded and extinguished. The disk was once again covered only with smeared blood and oil.

Outside, the ocean was still. Nubon clenched her blade, wrested from the bones of the god's messenger. The salt of the ocean was that of her blood. The thunder of the waves was the thrum of her heartbeat. And the billow of her lungs, the wind of the rising Tempest.

MEN OF DISTANT SOULS

R. T. DONLON

About R. T. Donlon

R.T. Donlon spends his mornings with coffee in hand and computer open to his next novel in progress. He is a high school teacher by day, a basketball coach by night, and an author everywhere in between. He is the author of a zombie-tale thriller called *Walls*, a supernatural fantasy novel called *The Reaper Trials*, and now, a 12-part fantasy epic called *The Edge of a New Beginning: Book I of the City of Shadow & Dust* Series.

He can be found at his website as well as on Facebook, Twitter, and Instagram.

www.rtdonlon.com

MEN OF DISTANT SOULS

The spattering first drops of rainwater tapped the window glass of Opie's Tavern. The storm rolling in had sent most scrambling back to their homes, especially this late on a Tuesday evening.

But not Levi.

The stubble across the sides of his face had grown into something more like patchwork shrubbery, each individual hair clawing its way out of his face from cheeks to his upper lip. He scratched at it with just-long-enough fingernails, lined with dirt from days of picking through dumpsters, piles of uneaten food and restaurant debris. He wore a torn tee shirt the color of the Atlantic Ocean four miles out from shore and a pair of jeans smeared with something you would see caked to the underbelly of a thirty-year-old subway turnstile.

So, Levi clutched at his beer with tense fingers, protecting those last few ounces of alcohol as though it were his first-born child. He took a sip every minute or so, savoring the bitter pull of it against his tongue. He had to make the best of it. It would be his last glass of the night.

"You've been milkin' that beer for an hour, Levi," the bartender said, drying his hands against a dirty towel. "It won't get you drunker just lookin' at it."

Levi peered up from his hunched posture behind the bar, lifting his eyes to the bartender as if he had never seen the man before.

"This is as sober as I've been all day," said Levi. "I'm out of money."

He twirled the cup between his thumb and index finger, watching the foam swirl, then trickle against the glass.

"Screw it," Levi whispered as he downed the rest of it.

"Last call," the bartender said, sending the glass under the bar for cleaning. "Sure I can't interest you in one more?"

Levi's eyes widened.

"I'll take it if you're givin' it."

"Sorry, Levi," the bartender continued. "No pay. No give."

Levi smiled, prying himself from the seat he had been plastered to for the last three hours.

"Well," he continued. "I think that's my cue."

"I'll buy him one."

The voice had carried over the bell that signaled a new entrant to the bar. This man—a slender one wearing a black suitcoat, a gray V-neck shirt, and black slacks—strolled toward Levi with a twenty-dollar bill overhead.

"Last call, pal," the bartender grunted.

The twenty-dollar bill found its way to the bar top, sliding to the edge of the wood so that the bartender could see it clearly against the tinny light filtering through the lamps above their heads. The bartender stared at the money for a few egregious moments, then whisked it away into his pocket.

"One drink," he accepted.

"Thank you," the new man smirked. "I'm sure my friend here will enjoy that."

"Thanks," Levi turned, "but I ain't no friend."

The barkeep slid a glass of frothy ale in front of each of them. The new entrant took a dainty sip from the head, while Levi hoisted into a hearty swig. He hadn't expected to feel the warmth of yet another buzz, but he swore he could feel it rising to his skull in short order.

"Will there be sleep out there for you tonight?" the mysterious man asked.

Levi rested the glass against the bar top and turned. His appearance must have given his homelessness away.

"There is always sleep," replied Levi, "just not the kind I want."

The man held out a hand, angling it across the table so that Levi's eyes directed toward it.

"The name's Daener," the man introduced himself. "Max Daener."

Levi held out his own hand in response. The dirt underneath his fingernails suddenly ashamed him, but Daener did not seem to care. Instead, the man took Levi's hand with force, shaking it firmly for a solid three seconds. It was only then that Levi offered his own name.

"So," Daener continued, taking another sip of his ale, "you've been unlucky for so long. Aren't you sick of living this kind of life?"

Levi rose a bit from his hunched posture, curving into the curiosity behind Daener's question.

"Do I have any other choice?" Levi asked.

At this, Daener cracked the corner of his mouth into a grin. It was the kind of grin that seemed to be suppressing ulterior motives and now, since the man had made his intentions a bit more apparent, Levi narrowed his eyes into a moderately-focused squint.

"You see," Daener began, "there is more to this place than you think. You've been living with the idea that this is all you've been given. I'm here to tell you—" Daener trailed off, his voice dying into an echo of itself. Levi waited for him to continue, but nothing came.

"Tell me what?" Levi continued, but the curiosity of Daener's distant voice brought on a slew of other questions Levi simply couldn't answer.

"I don't think you're ready for what I am about to tell you," the man continued.

Levi, for the first time all day, forgot about the half-empty beer in front of him and directed his full attention to Max, who continued staring intently into the color of his nearly full glass of ale.

"Tell me," Levi demanded.

"You must prove yourself first," Daener smiled. "I haven't made up my mind if I like you yet."

There was a quick moment of silence, then another moment filled with Levi's impatient huffing. He didn't know why his curiosity had suddenly gotten the best of him, but in some strange way, it felt right, natural.

"Answer me a question," Daener continued, "and I'll tell you what you so desperately want to hear."

Levi downed the rest of his ale and wiped the back of his hand across his dirty mustache.

"You've seen me before," Daener whispered. "Where?"

"What kind of question is that?" Levi pushed back. "I've never seen you before in my—"

But there was something about that dark, quiet smirk that sent a shiver of memory through the neurons of Levi's drunk brain. He had seen this man's face before! He had! But where? Levi closed his eyes, pushing his lids hard against his upturned cheekbones. Flashes of images scattered the emptiness behind his eyes. He saw nothing, thought nothing, felt nothing....

"You're trying too hard," Daener whispered. "You won't remember anything with that sort of concentration."

When Levi opened his eyes, Daener had already opened the bar door and stepped out into the rain-soaked sidewalk of a February night in the city. Levi, almost instinctually, panicked, jettisoned from the barstool and followed the man out into the cold. He could not believe that Daener had left so quickly, with unfinished business no less! The man had started something curious and goddamn it if he would leave it open-ended.

"Stop following me, Levi," the man spoke from a ways in front. "You have nothing to offer me."

"You can't just leave like that," Levi persisted. "You started something—"

Daener turned hard from his cantor-like walk, stopping in a dead halt.

"Do you remember?" he asked. "Do you?"

Levi stood half-dazed from the alcohol, perplexed by the man's sudden direction. He attempted to speak, but his mouth had zapped any sort of moisture from making that happen.

"If it hasn't happened now, it's not going to," Daener growled, "so leave. You're not who I'm looking for."

"…The bridge. You were standing on the bridge with your arms in front of you. You wanted me to go with you, but I couldn't. It was a long walk and the rain had already taken its toll on me. That was a bad night. I was sick for weeks."

Daener stood with his shoulders unhinged, releasing the impatient tension running across the muscles at the base of his neck. Something changed in his demeanor. He seemed liberated, freed from the shackles of uncertainty.

"Good," he said. "I guess you are not as useless as I thought you were."

Breathing heavily, Levi stepped forward. He did not know why he felt so compelled to follow this man, but something within him told him he must, like a magnet attracted to a piece of metal.

"I don't know what you want from me," Levi mumbled, "but I want to know."

"You want to know," Daener replied, although it was not nearly enough inflection for a question.

Levi nodded.

"Good," Daener whispered. "Follow me."

◆

The evening wind was no ordinary wind. It seemed to curve and sway to meet Levi's face, exposed to the elements against the edges of his coat's collar. He tried to cover it, but it was no use. His nose had taken on a red hue and had begun to dribble tiny runnels of mucous. His eyes watered against the wind's bitter swell and he blinked to push them away.

The two men had been walking for an extraordinarily long time.

"Where are you taking me?" Levi finally asked.

The silence had been secretly killing him, but for the sake of propriety, he kept his impatient and stubborn thoughts to himself.

"You will find out soon," Daener replied.

They had walked for at least three miles through city street after city street until they reached an alleyway blocked by a crooked, rusted chained fence and a series of pivoted dumpsters. Daener stopped abruptly in front of one of the cleaner dumpsters and leaned against its chipping green paint.

"I possess the ability to show you something you have never seen before," Daener began. "Something that, once you've seen it, will change you. I will show it only if you accept my invitation."

The demand was almost formal, but not entirely clear. A vague interest perked the corners of the words and, suddenly, Levi felt uneasy.

"I've come this far," Levi began, "chasing a man I have never really met. Do you play me for a fool?"

Levi waited for a response, but the deadpan expression plastered to Daener's already mute face silenced him for yet another few seconds.

"You must say that you accept," Daener confirmed.

And so Levi did.

"Welcome," Daener said, pushing away one of the dumpsters as he spoke, "to your new beginning."

Levi held a hand to his eyes. In the dusky dark of the outer metropolis, he had to squint to keep his vision from failing. He could only decipher the silhouette of a door somewhere within the thirty to fifty-foot distance deeper into the alleyway.

"A door?" Levi asked. "Where does it lead?"

He scanned the buildings to the left and right of the passageway, but found nothing in terms of immediate signage. The broken windows to the left and the graffiti vandalism to the right told Levi all he needed to know—these buildings had been abandoned some time ago.

"Go ahead," Daener urged. "You will never know until you try."

What the hell are you doing? Levi thought. *Is this a trap? Why would Daener do such a thing to someone like me? But then there's the whole thing with the remembering….How could I remember something like the bridge….*

Cautiously, Levi stepped toward the door. Daener watched quietly from his leaned-in position against the dumpster. The air compacted around Levi, making it harder to breathe as he approached.

It was ordinary—a marbled wood finish with no windows and a bronze doorknob just big enough to clutch with a closed fist. Nothing stood out at Levi in the darkness except for one peculiar scratch that ran from the top right panel to a gorged chip in the center of the bottom left. To most, this diagonal cut in the wood may not even have been noticed, but to Levi, it presented an entirely new level of concern. It had been used over and over again for some time now.

"What's behind this door?" he asked.

The silhouette of Daener only shrugged, shoving his hands in his pockets.

"You will only know," Daener pushed, "if you open it."

As if the words had sent his hand to the door, Levi's fingers clasped the doorknob, twisting it against the weight of his wrist. The door creaked open, sending a sliver of sunlight breaking from the crack and illuminating the side of the nearest building. He swung the door open and, unbelieving, caught his own breath at the base of his throat.

"It can't be," Levi whispered. "How can this—" His voice trailed off, deafened by the onslaught of passing thoughts in his brain.

"There are a thousand different worlds just like this one—worlds where you could have had a full, peaceful life—but for some reason, fate chose for you to suffer, to live out your days on the streets of a rundown city," Daener continued.

Levi breathed heavily, admiring the sunlit field behind the door, stretching far into the distance.

"This can't be real," Levi mumbled.

"It's as real as the air you're breathing now. It's as real as the asphalt under your feet. It's as real as you are."

Levi took a step forward only to be met by Daener's firm hand.

"Be forewarned," the man spoke. "Once you have left this world, you may never return. Only the Mediators know how to travel from place to place and I, for one, will not grant you that power. You have been offered a gift—one that has the ability to change the life you have previously led. It is now your decision to leave this life behind or stay and accept what could have been."

Levi allowed his options to creep through his mind, but this was an easy decision. There was nothing left for him here.

"I've made up my mind," said Levi. "Let's go."

Max Daener grinned through the controlled stretching of his face, then ushered Levi to the sunlit door.

"Go," said Daener. "May your next life be better than the last."

The doorway sent a shock through Levi's system. For the briefest of moments, it felt as though a giant vacuum had sucked every last bit of air from his body, pressing him into nothing but a flat wafer of mashed skin and bone. When he emerged on the other side, he immediately felt the warmth of sunlight bathe his skin. There was energy there that he had not felt in such a long time and it brought him a sense of comfort—not relief in its entirety, but a sense of it.

When he turned, the doorway portal had vanished.

"Max?" he called out, but he heard no reply. He tried again, but only the chirping of birds rang true from the wood to his right. Both an anxious and calming feeling closed on him. He felt the need to run, to find civilization, to make his life's purpose clear again, but also, he felt a new need to sit amidst the tall, angling stalks of grass and think about what the magnitude of what he had just done.

"Holy shit," he whispered to himself. "Did I just—" But he couldn't finish his own thought. Instead, he decided to force his legs to move, to start new.

For miles, he walked until he discovered a dirt path stretching over hills of overgrown weeds and patches of lush grass. He followed it into a valley town expelling plumes of thick, gray smoke from several chimneys at the center of a town square. The smoke dispersed into ribbons as it floated to the sky, then disappeared into the blue just above his head.

He watched as figures below walked from building to building in a hurry, carrying heavy objects with only the strength of their arms. They seemed rushed, almost panicked, but normal in every other sense of being human. He thought about calling down to them and went so far as to lift his hands to his mouth for amplification, but rescinded his choice at the last minute. Calling out would only startle them and, assuming their already tense state of being, Levi decided to climb down and join the foray himself.

The dirt path wound down the hill, descending straight into the valley until it opened up into townlands a few meters from the first standing structure—a barn erected from lumber and tree bark. It stood about fifteen feet high and twenty feet across. A charred crater in the earth hid behind it, lurking like an empty eye socket in the ground. A thick layer of ash covered the ground in a fifty-foot radius surrounding the pit and, as it appeared to Levi, seemed to be a symbol of something terrible, something traumatizing.

"Excuse me," a quiet voice spoke from behind him. "Who...who are you?"

Levi turned to find a child peering up at him from a distance. He wore a torn, beige shirt that hung from his shoulders like a rag from a clothesline. He wore jeans but the left leg had been ripped away at the knee. Without a belt, the boy's skinny hips could barely hold the fabric at his waist and, every few seconds, the boy's hands clutched at his pockets and hiked the jeans up to keep them level. The look on his face showed fear in its most common form.

"I'm not going to hurt you," Levi said.

The city's cold from behind the portal-door had not altogether left Levi's face, shading the curves of his nose and cheekbones with a dull flush of red. To an outsider, Levi must have appeared to be something like an alien, wearing his dirtied pants, two-layered jacket, and ragged shoes.

"Then why are you sneaking behind the barn?" the boy asked.

"I came from the fields over there," Levi continued, pointing west. "A man named Max Daener brought me here."

The child bowed his head slightly, processing. This was an adult conversation for which he was not prepared. In a moment of panic, the boy pivoted and sprinted into the town square.

"Wait!" Levi called. "Don't run!"

His legs carried him through an intermingling of buildings, chasing the boy into the town square where hundreds of eyes stared at him with wide expressions. He stopped, skidding across the dirt pathway in his sole-less shoes. Something felt terrible about this group of people. Something felt empty, disparaging.

"Intruder!" one of the men whispered from the backside of the group. His voice barely carried over the lines of men, women, and children in front of him.

"Are you one of them?" another man asked.

This one stood front and center with his arm wrapped around a shaking woman to his left.

"One of who?" Levi asked.

The man paused for the briefest of moments, scanned the confusion in Levi's face, then answered.

"Them. The ones that made the pit."

"I was brought here by a man named Max Daener. I came through a portal from the fields over there."

The crew of men and women bowed their heads almost simultaneously, shrouding their eyes in a cloud of shadows. From left to right, murmurings of disgruntled and confused questions filled the air. Levi's heartbeat quickened.

"Is Daener one of yours?"

The people almost quivered when Levi asked the question, which exposed another bit of perplexity within him.

"I've never heard of that name," one of the grungier men said.

"Me either!" said another.

"None of us have," another called from the back of the mob.

"We do know who you are," a strong man interjected from the far left.

The speaking man wore a rather scraggly beard that had just begun falling from his jaw. His brown eyes accentuated the brown streaks of hair against an otherwise black sea of directionless strands that fell from all angles across his scalp. In his right hand, he carried an axe. The left was empty.

"They talk about you all the time," the man continued. "You're the one they want. You're the one they've been waiting for."

Levi's heart quickened yet again. It felt as though it were bulging from his chest in a mess of uncoordinated fibrillations.

"These people," Levi probed. "How do they know me?"

"They are not people," the man continued. "They are as far from human as anything can be."

"They call us the Mediators!" interjected a new voice.

The crowd separated into two distinct pockets while a single person emerged from the path down their middle. He walked casually—putting one foot gently in front of the other—allowing the sunlight to break free and expose his face.

"Daener," Levi whispered. "You're here!"

"Bringing you here was no simple task. It took years upon years to construct the perfect conditions. I didn't think you would accept the call."

"The call?" Levi asked.

"We needed you here," Daener continued, "because you have something very special within you, something we need."

Levi's hesitation forced a devious smile to filter through Daener's strangely thin mouth. The expression across Levi's face must have told him everything he wanted to know.

"That face," Daener continued, "is the face of a man who knows he's been played."

The moments that had led up to his decision to follow Daener into that alley, to be persuaded by the man's charm, to open that scratched door amid the city's shadows suddenly felt disgustingly artificial, as though he had just awoken from a particularly awful night tremor. Daener watched this realization flood Levi's face, absorbing disbelief like oxygen dissolving into the confines of his lungs.

"If I'm to be honest," Daener continued, "it was never supposed to be so…prolonged. You were just so damn stubborn."

"Whatever it is you need from me," Levi barked, "I won't surrender it. Not to the likes of you. Why would you do this to me?"

There was a moment of disdain on Daener's face, then as if it were completely normal to have your face melt away in a layer of beige-colored ooze, Levi watched as Daener devolved into something new, something terrifying. What used to be skin had taken on a black residue, stretched to its limits by cords of overworked, veiny muscles. His eyes filled with black, stretching over the white tissue of his eyeballs. Only a thin circle of white now surrounded his massive pupils. His previously straight-lined, perfect teeth morphed into thousands of miniature daggers, inching forward from his mouth in a tilted, outward angle. Fingernails grew several inches into chipped knives clawing at the air from outstretched fingers.

In a display of maddening speed, Daener burst forward and tackled Levi to the ground with ease.

"We will take what we need," Daener growled, lifting a clawed hand to Levi's chest.

He felt the life drain from him in a moment of vulnerability as a string of vibrant energy rose from the center of his chest, pulling him up toward the monster on top of him. Daener wrapped it around the palm of his hand like a cord of rope, admiring it.

"The hero soul," Daener whispered. "At last! It is here!"

It took every ounce of Levi's remaining energy to breathe, to grunt against the ripping pain in his chest. The hero soul, as Daener called it, felt as though it were evaporating any sort of emotion or feeling he had ever felt. There was an increasing hollowness within him now that had never existed before. It horrified him.

"Good," Daener said, smiling through his rows of jagged teeth. "You're already accepting it, aren't you?"

"Accepting what?" Levi grunted, gurgling hard against the pain.

Daener unraveled the hero soul from his palm, allowing it to snap back into Levi's chest. Thoughts, memories, emotions, and feelings quickly returned to him in a flood of colors.

"Fate," the monster whispered.

"What did you do to me?" Levi barked, squirming out of the grasp of the monster.

"Fear not, Levi. The strength of the soul has not yet reached its full power. You are safe for now."

Daener smiled in a strange, thousand-tooth kind of way.

"The hero soul reincarnates every ten thousand years," the monster continued. "It is hard to find…and even harder to harvest," Daener explained, "and yet, it is the source of all the Realms. As long as the hero soul lives, so will humanity. The best part? It's living in you."

The look in Levi's eyes surfaced as nothing less than sheer terror.

"You see? I didn't do this to you," the monster continued. "It's been in you since your moment of conception. It's been planned for generation upon generation before you. You are just one cog in the macrocosm of the multiverse. An important cog, for sure, but a cog, nonetheless."

Something changed in Levi, something drastic. His eyes shimmered through a different sort of quietness. His mouth quivered a tiny bit less. Even the weary lines of too many drunken, wasteful years quietly disappeared. He could feel his muscles growing under his skin. His heart pumped less wildly behind a stronger ribcage.

"There it is," Daener smiled. "Though you will try and fight it, the hero will emerge in you. And when it does…"

The Mediator turned, stretching the ropes of muscle that coiled against its blackened skin.

"…I'll be back for it."

The crowd of watching people, paralyzed by the Mediator's presence, fell backwards against Daener's sudden takeoff. The monster propelled into the sky—a wake of black soot-smoke stretching into directional waves. In a matter of seconds, Daener had left their field of vision, vanishing like the sun after dusk.

Levi turned to the crowds surrounding him. They stared at him differently now, more in admiration than in fear. Slowly, they began to turn to each other, whispering only two words repeatedly over and over.

"The hero," they chanted. "The hero."

◆

The meal he ate in the Braddenburroughs two days ago had begun cramping his stomach into a fury of knots, so naturally, he cursed those underwhelming cooks repeatedly under his breath until he reached Annistown. He had hopes of making it to a facility before then, but it had not played out that way. Instead, he found himself sickened with the strain of the Poison Meat disease floating around these parts of Six.

"I knew I shouldn't have touched the lamb," he mumbled to himself, struggling against another bout of queasiness.

A flow of vomit pounced at him like a stray cat.

"Better hole up here for the night," he grunted, swiveling his eyes to an alcove just outside the edge of the Traveler's Road.

Levi gathered brush for a makeshift fire, rolled out his sleeping mat so that it paralleled the heat of the flames, and sat back against a tree to watch the sunlight dwindle at the horizon line in the distance. The way the sun died had always seemed magical here, reflecting perfectly against the green and brown hues of the fields and forests between the interlocking townlands. The cities and pockets of smog from his time in Forty-Seven made it hard to enjoy even a glimmer of what he knew now and, every day, he thanked the Mediator Daener for what beautiful gift he had given him.

But the generosity stopped there.

He learned the true stories of the Mediators some time ago and what the hero soul truly meant to the people of the Realms. The truth was, he had to see it for himself to believe it. In each Realm, there are a thousand hidden portals—each to another Realm in those Thousand. With the Mediators in the wind for so long, Levi left the comfort of Cypress and embarked on a journey to discover the worlds he had never known existed.

Only the Mediators can travel between Realms, Daener had told him, and I am not willing to relinquish that power to you.

But Levi had found a few of these portals and discovered he could, in fact, travel through. Those few worlds he dared to find sent chills down his spine, the worst being an apocalyptic landscape at the heart of Thirty.

"The Mediators," a dying woman spoke weakly from her view just outside of the city. Burns had turned most of her body to a charred remnant of itself. "They took everything. Everything."

"Why?" Levi asked.

But it was too late. She had closed her eyes, gasped one last time, and went limp. Levi left Thirty with a sharp pang in his heart and a black mark stained to his soul. The Realms could only take so much of this destruction and—since Levi had embarked on this journey—he had seen too much of it to accept his place in Six. The Realms needed him.

And a hero he would need to be.

So, it was here that he thought about these things. The roaring fire sent warmth across him in waves and, for the first time in a long time, Levi settled into a state of comfort. He ripped into the flesh of an apple, chewing slowly to savor the sugar against his tongue. He had lost a lot of food (and money) upchucking that wasted reek of Braddenburrough stew, so the apple was a nice cleanse of his otherwise abused palette. When he finished, he threw the core over his shoulder and listened to it thud behind him in a mess of shrubs. He settled down into the sleeping mat and closed his eyes. As he began drifting into the unconscious, the subtle sound of a snapping twig thrust him back into reality.

"I can't believe it," a male voice whispered from behind the shadows of the fire. "You are—"

"I am not who you think I am," Levi interrupted in a half-hearted grumble.

The voice halted to a near stop, then slowly, against a bout of clearing his throat, began again.

"It's okay," the man said. "You're not in danger."

At this, Levi pushed himself from the mat, still bitter at sleep interrupted.

They all say that, Levi thought.

"That's a first," he said out loud, turning toward the visitor. "I wasn't expecting any company tonight."

"It seems the Realms would see us together tonight," the man continued. "You can't barter with fate, I'd imagine."

There was something too convivial in this traveler's words, something too warm.

No one, thought Levi, stumbled upon anything these days.

And yet, Levi offered the traveler the benefit of the doubt, ushering the man to the fire with a quick, but welcoming gesture.

"Come," Levi grumbled. "Sit."

The man approached and reclined against a withered log at his back. He possessed, quite possibly, the broadest shoulders Levi had ever seen. Behind metal plates of armor, those thick blankets of muscle crept to a slew of biceps and triceps that bulged against wristlet chainmail and dirtied roamer's glovers. He wore a slender bit of armor that dangled against the push of his chest. His pants showed stains of bloodshed, hopefully that of animals, but Levi kept his sword close to his open palm just in case.

"Do you happen to have any food? Any water? I've been on the road for days and have found nothing—"

Before the man could finish his sentence, Levi tossed an apple in the direction of the man. He caught it with a quick flash of reflexes. He had pawned six apples from a road merchant a few miles back and figured the least he could do was repay the karmic forces of the Realms by giving back.

"Thanks," the man said, sinking his yellow teeth into the apple's skin. "The name's Bodin. Bodin Falswear."

"Termean Hall," Levi lied. "Pleasure's mine."

The man's face tilted toward the firelight, exposing his harsh, road-warrior features. The stubble across his jaw ran in spotty patches, mostly against several scars that had healed and pinked against the otherwise tan, aged skin. His eyes glowed hazel, but one sagged more than the other. This man—Bodin Falswear—had been through many battles, Levi thought, some that left him in in pretty rough shape.

"You don't have to play games with me," Bodin said. "I know who you are. The whole world knows who you are."

Levi chuckled at this. Without knowing it, this man had offered up his only play…and for what? Common decency?

"So," Levi smirked. "You know me? From where, may I ask?"

The man quietly inched forward.

"Word of mouth, of course. You can't travel from here to Witterdom without hearing of the name Levi Folsom—the vessel of the hero soul. You're practically legend!"

Bodin's voice had carried across the darkening landscape, resonating through the forested hills in the distance. Immediately, he sank back against the tree apologetically. Perhaps Levi was as recognizable as Bodin said he was.

You'll have to disguise yourself a bit better next time, Levi thought.

Another snap of teeth against apple catalyzed a second spurt of conversation.

"So," Bodin continued, "where is the great Levi Folsom headed?"

Levi considered the question.

"Annistown, among other places," Levi mumbled.

The sleep that had crept into his eyes had dimmed his mind into slumber, but with a quick shake the haze fluttered into the night. He could see the full scale of the man now, how monstrous he truly was, extending from scarred face all the way to the steeled armor across the tops of his feet. The half-eaten apple rolled across the man's fingertips in a circular sway, playing as he bit, allowing its juice to run from the corners of his mouth to the patchy bulge of his chin.

"Annistown is just a few clicks east of here," Bodin continued. "Is there a reason you stopped?"

There was a hint of intent behind the question, as if Bodin wished Levi to realize it.

"Stew hit me in ways I wish it hadn't," Levi answered.

Silently, Levi's fingers clutched tighter around the hilt of his sword.

"No," Bodin continued. "I don't buy it. There's something in Annistown, isn't there? Something you're after."

The convivial appearance washed away into a shadow left only by something evil, something plagued.

"I'm just a journeyman, sir," Levi grumbled. "Nothing more."

At first, Bodin's movements dimmed the fire to a shell of itself, embers bubbling a faint orange against the ashes , but then, as Bodin reached for Levi's throat with tense fingers, the flames roared back to power, licking the air in whips of heat. With an upward thrust, Bodin lifted Levi from the ground by his neck.

So, he possesses the bandit soul, Levi thought.

There was no panic in Levi's thoughts, no knots of fear in his abdomen.

"You're making…a grave…mistake," Levi gurgled. "Put…me down."

Levi reached for Bodin's grip, but could not shake him away.

"I can't believe my luck!" Bodin grunted. "The hero soul! In my presence, no less!"

Enough games, Levi thought, ripping his sword from its sheath. He slashed it across his body so that it cut Bodin's arm clean off midway to the elbow. One spurt of blood shot from the wound and, suddenly, the man's mind caught up to the shock of the moment. He screamed a bellowing jolted scream and fell to his knees.

Levi, on the other hand, had landed on his feet. Trickles of red dripped from the tip of his sword's blade, now at his side.

"Bring them out," said Levi. "Bandits like you never travel alone."

At first, Bodin hesitated, but the blade of Levi's sword to his neck propelled him into acceptance.

"Come out!" Bodin screamed. "Just do it!"

Six bodies emerged from the darkness, each holding swords, spears, and shields against tense arms.

"No need to be scared," Levi continued. "You've asked for this. Your man here is proof."

The pale look of a man losing too much blood replaced Bodin's previously fearless demeanor. The wound at the end of his shortened arm oozed uncontrollably. Bodin turned to the fire, reaching the stub of his arm toward it. Levi stopped him with the tip of his blade.

"No," Levi whispered. "You haven't earned the privilege to save yourself."

The six figures in the distance approached, growing larger against the roaring fire while the pallor of Bodin's face worsened.

"You will die if you don't cauterize that wound in the next few minutes," explained Levi. "Tell your crew to drop their weapons and join me in the light. Do it now or I will let you die."

"Fine!" screamed Bodin. "Bandits, lay down your arms!"

"Your people," continued Levi, "have given you a special opportunity—one that will benefit, not only me, but you, as well."

The five men and one woman of Bodin's crew revealed themselves to the light of the fire. Each had similar scars running over their coarse faces. Some were missing patches of hair. Others had been swathed in bandages across limbs now seeping blood.

"Closer," Levi ushered. "Don't be afraid. Closer."

The men and woman did as they were told, inching closer until Levi rushed forward, sending his sword deep into the heart of each bandit in a flash of speed. The last several attempted to scamper away into the fields before Levi turned on them, but the hero was too quick.

Bodin cried out in shock as the bodies fell in bloody sprays to the ground.

"They have not died in vain, Bodin. They have died so that you, indeed, may live," Levi continued. "But there is part of the story you were never told about the hero soul—a tale that will change the way you look at me. It is a tale that you will wish you had heard before you decided to ambush me."

Bodin's breathing went choppy. Blood trickled from the corner of his mouth as he coughed.

"The hero soul," explained Levi, "is much more than an idea. It's a presence. Sometimes it fuels me, controls me. When my body is in peril, as you decided to trigger a few minutes ago, it takes over and forces me to do things— like what I have done to your band of merry brothers. And then," Levi continued, holding his hand over the corpses, "I do this."

The mouths of the bandits snapped open. From each, a wispy string of energy illuminating their dead skin, slipped from their teeth and slithered like earthworms through mud. They zipped through the air to Levi's chest, which opened into a display of blinding lights. Suddenly, Levi appeared stronger, less wrinkled around the eyes, broader around the shoulders, and fewer strands of gray blended into his beard.

The hero dropped into a low squat, still holding the sword, although relaxed now.

"You see," the hero continued, "the soul has given me unique abilities. I never wanted this. In fact, sometimes I reflect on my previous life and wonder how easy it would have been just to surrender, but I was brought here by the Mediators…and only by the Mediators shall I be free."

Levi's demeanor turned serious.

"But every time you shards of gutter trash poke at me, the Mediators draw closer. I'm sick of it!"

He dropped his sword into the fire. The flames consumed the metal, running like water from edge to edge. Sparks rushed into the sky, then disappeared into blackened remnants. When the blade glowed a reddened shade of orange, Levi took the hilt and held it out to the stub of Bodin's bloody arm.

"This will hurt," he said.

The hiss was to be expected, but Bodin's shrill cry was not.

"You'll live," Levi whispered. "Get up."

When Bodin remained still, breathing heavily against the pain of his lack of an arm, Levi wrapped his fingers into a the bandit's hair and pulled him onto his feet. With a surly grunt, Bodin wavered upright to keep himself at eye level.

"You're going to do something for me," Levi continued, "and, if I hear that you're not, I will track you down and take your life as I have done to your friends. Understood?"

The barely-standing Bodin nodded, quietly gasping.

"You will cease your stealing. You will cease your meddling ways. You will travel from town to town and, when the townsfolk ask why you have no arm, you tell them the truth. You tell them Levi Folsom took it. You tell them the hero punished you for every bad thing you have ever done."

Bodin nodded once again, coughing against the mucous and blood puddling in his throat.

"I…I will…" he said.

"Good," Levi confirmed. "Now go. I hope, for your sake, I never see your face again."

Bodin stumbled across the fire's lackluster embers, tripping over the roots from the tree's stump behind him. He clutched at the bare base of his arm with the other, moving quietly into the darkness of the fields.

Levi slid down the bark of the tree until his ass found the dirt, reached into the pocket of his oversized cloak-jacket, and began shining an apple in preparation of another snack.

The sugar of its flesh tasted fresh against the back of his tongue.

◆

"Your arm!" a man from an open coffee shop yelled down the cobblestone street. "Hurry! Hurry! In you go."

Annistown had appeared in the distance—a sharp foray of shimmering firelights across a small lip of land. His vision had clouded into blurs of pain. His consciousness went in and out, reeling around fever-riddled moments of stumbling black-outs. It was only when he reached the town that he realized how truly desperate he was for help.

"Here," the café owner continued, placing a sturdy hand against his back. "Lie down."

Bodin barely crossed the café's threshold before collapsing onto the creaky wood floors. The café owner stood, frail and panicked. Unfortunately, the weight of Bodin proved to be too much, and the café owner lost him as he fell.

"What's your name?" the owner asked, kneeling beside Bodin's groaning body.

When the bandit didn't answer, he asked again, "What's your name? Look at me! You're going to be fine. Just focus."

But it was too late. Bodin could only groan against the pain of his absent arm.

Streaks of blood covered his armor, caked against the metal links of the chainmail. Several customers retreated from their tables to the back wall in fear.

"He's a bandit," a golden-haired, pale-skinned twenty-something spoke briskly.

"Errrr," Bodin grumbled.

He kept his eyes closed, lids pressed together.

"He needs a doctor," the owner said, panicked. "Someone! Get Carlson! Someone!"

The exposed wound at the end of Bodin's arm throbbed, still cooling from Levi's cauterizing. He reached for it every few seconds, but flinched when anything touched the open nerve endings, including the wind corralling itself through the entranceway. It felt as though his veins had filled with fire, pushing through his body to its very center.

"Carlson! Thank God!" the owner screamed in relief.

The doctor raced to Bodin's side, scanning him with cautious eyes. He worked primarily over the black-rimmed he wore on the bridge of his nose, but pushed them up with a quick jab every minute or so. His thinning brown hair appeared as though it had been sculpted hours before, but now, sat disarrayed after a long day that had somehow just been stretched even longer.

"What happened?" Carlson asked. "Who knows this man?"

It wasn't until the doctor peered up from his work on the wound that anyone dared to answer him.

"He stumbled his way in from the fields," the owner continued. "He's dressed like a...a..."

"A bandit," the doctor confirmed. "It's okay. You can say it."

The owner shivered at the sound of the word. Its coarse touch against his ears sent a tingling sensation to the corners of his mouth.

"Their stronger souls make it easier for them to heal, but this wound is bad. Someone got him good," explained the doctor. "I'm guessing this wasn't an accident."

The loss of blood still had Bodin feeling extremely weak, so much so that he found that he could not pry himself from the floorboards. He could, however, grunt a few lines before the fluid in his lungs took over yet again.

"It was Levi Folsom," Bodin coughed. "It was."

Several of the café dwellers that had retreated into the shadows gasped. Levi Folsom had somehow become a household name—a terror, a treasure, a savior to the Sixth. Bodin raised the dried stub to the doctor and grimaced.

"He told me to tell everyone what he did," Bodin continued. "He told me this was the punishment for all the bad things I've done."

Of course, this wasn't the entire story, but the Annistown citizens didn't have to know that.

"He is not who we think he is. He's a monster!" Bodin gurgled, coughing back a slew of emotions.

A clack-clack of boots turned the attention of all to the entranceway. A bearded man in a black cloak-jacket walked in, sword in sheath. Bodin's eyes immediately grew wide. He squirmed against the doctor's firm grip, retreating in paranoia.

"It's him!" Bodin cried. "It's Folsom!"

The back-wall observers squirmed unpleasantly. The café owner stood quietly against the shelves of flavored coffees. The doctor peered up through his spectacles, squinting at the man towering above him.

"Excuse me, doctor," Levi spoke calmly. "I have to ask you to step away from my friend, here."

The tension flooding the room intensified. For a few moments, the only sound was the sound of pounding hearts in the throats of all.

Except Levi's.

"If you do not want to witness what comes next," Levi spoke calmly, "I suggest you leave now. Go home. Forget what you have seen here."

He offered a moment for processing, then nodded as no one left.

"Very well," he continued. "Brace yourselves."

"Wait!" Bodin screamed. "Wait! I can explain!"

"There has been enough explanation. I offered you one chance and, as I thought, you squandered it. You are a true bandit, Bodin. You should die that way."

Levi lifted the sword out of its sheath and wrapped both hands around the hilt. The blade shimmered against the lamplight,. He peered down at Bodin, almost relishing these last few moments of fear in the bandit's eyes. The hero soul loved these moments, but it terrified Levi, so when the blade slid through Bodin's chest and crushed the ribs protecting his heart, turmoil ran clear through Levi's consciousness.

A petite squeal broke from the back of the room. It was a sound that told of something that could not be unseen—an earthquake-like tremor of truth that resonated through the entire space.

Blood seeped from the wound in Bodin's chest. He choked from the weight of his own drowning, eyes wide and panicked as oxygen disappeared from his lungs in waves.

"It will be over quickly. Don't fight it. Shhh…"

The choking gasps devolved into gurgling spats of coughs. Those coughs quieted into the faint jerks of a drowning man. Seconds passed, then silence. Levi slid the sword from Bodin's chest, wiped the edge of the blade with a nearby cloth, and sheathed it yet again.

A pool of blood surrounded the bandit. If it weren't for the bloody body and the squealing woman in the back of the room, the deathly silence would have resembled a normal evening in the Annistown café. Instead, the men and women present stared at Levi with gaping eyes.

"You…" Carlson spoke, breaking the silence. "You killed him."

"I did what needed to be done. Do not judge. You wouldn't understand," Levi grumbled.

"What kind of crime can possibly justify killing a man? Executing him on the floor of a public café in front of a dozen people?"

Levi hesitated for just a moment. The doctor made a good point. Perhaps he could have been a bit more reserved in the way he had handled things.

"I invited you to leave if you did not wish to be present for what I was about to do," Levi barked. "I invite you once again to do the same if you do not wish to witness what comes next."

The doctor turned to the others in the room, aghast. No one spoke another word.

"Very well," Levi said. "I suggest you keep your moral bullshit to yourself."

The hero hovered his palm just above the bandit's mouth. From the pooling, already-congealing blood at the back of the bandit's throat, the cord emerged.   "The life force in everyone has a particular sort of strength. Some more than others," Levi explained. "There are certain things the hero soul forces me to do— things I am not proud of. This is one of those things."

The bandit soul hovered majestically between its previous host and Levi's outstretched hand. It rolled and turned as if caught in a magnetic field. Levi admired it with harsh, loving eyes. A flick of his downturned wrist sent the quivering cord of bandit soul deep into Levi's chest. A flash of bright light emerged from the spot and, when the eyes of the men and women in the café adjusted, it was astoundingly clear that Levi had taken on an entirely new, relinquished persona.

His skin shone like honey in sunlight. Ropes of muscles wrapped under skin in valiant, bulging fashion. The broad angles of his shoulders pushed his arms outward, flexed against the balance of his torso. His hair had grown another inch so that it fell to his shoulders in the slightest waves of amber locks. Despite all of this, something felt terrifyingly wrong. Misplaced, lost.

"What is it?" the café owner asked. "What's wrong?"

Levi turned his open hand so that his palm faced his eyes. An odd sensation of losing control, of vulnerability, coursed through his veins, and forced his heart into quickened beats. This was not a sensation he had ever felt before. In fact, this was something he had dreaded from the moment he entered Six. This was what he feared from the moment Daener had divulged his true purpose—the purpose of the Mediators. With Bodin's bandit soul now joining the rest within him, the hero soul was now ready.

And now, they would return.

◆

It has been some time since we last spoke, the voice in Levi's head called.

Levi couldn't sleep. It had been hours since he had taken Bodin's life force. He had stayed in the café for as long as he could, attempting to console the people he had terrified until the owner closed the shop for the night. He had found the nearest inn—the Whittaker—and had paid in full for the smallest room on record. He had found the bed as soon as he walked through the door, but his mind simply could not find rest. He lay there with eyes wide, staring at a large crack in the wall jutting from the trim at the base of the floor.

At first he thought the voice in his head was his own—a simple internal mind trick—but when it cropped up again, Levi knew it was more than that.

You do remember me, don't you? the voice continued. Daener. Your dear, old friend. You know what time it is.

There was a sort of disbelief in the way Levi processed the voice. It felt as if it were coming from the depths of his own mind.

You're right, the voice continued. *The hero soul and the Mediators are deeply connected. So connected that we can read the thoughts of the collective. At all times.*

Levi's breath caught in his throat.

Ah! I can feel it—the fear within you. Now that you have triggered the hero soul's final energy pull, you've joined the ranks of the Mediators. We can feel you, Levi. We can feel what you have inside you. You're ready. We will take what is rightfully ours.

"And what happens when you do?" Levi asked.

He didn't know why the question had risen to his mouth, but it had.

The voice cackled in response.

One day, it whispered. *You have one day before we find you. We are everywhere. Soon your world will burn.*

Thunder broke in the deepest parts of his brain. The connection with Daener cut harshly and he was left abandoned inside his little room with nothing but the sound of the Annistown wind scratching at the dirty windowpane. For a moment, the anxiety within him attempted a full-system, full-body takeover, but within a series of breaths, he regained control of his thoughts.

"You can do this," Levi whispered to himself. "You've been planning for this for so long. It's time to finish it once and for all."

And yet, the tension constricting his chest told him otherwise.

The words of Max Daener kept clawing at the inside of his skull: *Your world will burn.*

Moments moved in blurs.

He bought a horse from a woman dressed like a rancher. She seemed sturdy enough to trust. Although it cost him most of his current stash, it was well worth it to shave the distance between Annistown and Cypress by three hours. He would return to his Sixth home in only a matter of hours now.

They would not be safe without him. It would be the first place the Mediators struck.

The darkening clouds in the distance had already started to form on the horizon. They raged quietly against the harsh eeriness of the full moon overhead.

The impending doom kept him at a rapid pace, despite the horse's constant resistance and, when they finally reached the little village of

Cypress, the storms had already filled the sky. The small cluster of buildings seemed empty, but Levi knew better. The citizens of Cypress did many things well, but hiding from the real dangers of Six and beyond seemed to be their specialty.

"Cypress!" Levi screamed. "Come out!"

Hundreds of villagers slowly surfaced from every door and seal. A sense of relief flooded him. Months had passed since he had last seen them and now, in this moment, he realized just how much he had truly missed them. These people had accepted him when he had barged into Six as a man with no home. He would have to find it within himself to save that same home they had offered him that day.

"It's Levi!" a fragile elderly man yelled. "Levi is back!"

The hero tried to calm the sea of excitement that had suddenly began to surge, but he did so without any luck. Minutes passed before Levi held his hands over his head in frustration, signaling for the villagers to quiet themselves. That seemed to work. The crowd shushed almost instantly, but as the men, women, and children collected themselves, it was the dire expression riddling Levi's otherwise tense frame that truly changed the scope of Cypress' perception.

"What is it, Levi?" a man named Corgin asked from a distance. "Why have you returned?"

The hero's eyes naturally turned to the sky and the raging storms overhead.

"You have been preparing for this," Levi projected, talking as if they already knew. "Just as I have."

The faces of the crowd suddenly dropped.

"Why now?" Corgin asked. "Levi, what have you done?"

Levi dropped his eyes to the dirt-caked boots strapped handsomely to his feet. They had been good boots, made to last the treacherous landscapes of a Six journeyman. A single raindrop fell in that moment of reflection, splattering across his leather toe.

Then another.

And another, until the tiny thudding sounds of a thousand droplets dampened the dirt on which the crowd stood.

"I returned because you are not safe. The Mediators know what you all mean to me. They know what you have done to make me feel at home. It is not what I have done to bring this upon you," Levi continued. "It's how I will stop it."

The rain made it nearly impossible to hear the next question Corgin asked, yet Levi heard it as clear as the chirping of a bird on a summer's morning.

"And how do you propose you'll do that?"

Levi stepped forward, closing the gap between himself and the crowd of people he loved so dearly.

"By being what you all believe I am," he replied. "A hero."

◆

The people of Cypress filed away into their hiding nooks. The village buildings stood shadowed against the blankets of rain tumbling from the skies. Darkness consumed the land. It rolled across the hills behind him and blinded him from the mountains in the distance. Six had never been so bleak.

Levi closed his eyes. The rush of cold water trickling down his hair ran to the back of his neck where it soaked the cloak-jacket through. The sounds of a harsh wind caught hold of his ears, refusing to let go. The strange taste of metal rose to the base of his throat—the taste of anxiousness, nervous excitement.

"I know you're here," he projected. His voice trailed off against the storm. "Show yourselves. It's time to end this."

A hundred or so blackened bodies emerged in front of him, in line with the town square. Lines of them broke through the rain, smiling white with lines of pointed teeth. A strange hissing noise accompanied their entrance. Coils of claws and muscles moved in synchronicity, forever joined together as the collective they were.

I can feel it, a voice rang clear in Levi's head. The hero soul…

"And it is strong," said Levi. "I've trained it to be so."

The one Levi knew as Daener stepped forward, arching its back to turn toward the hero.

You knew this day would come, hero, Daener pushed. *You knew.*

"I did."

Then why do you resist? This is not your battle to be fought. You are merely the carrier.

"I am more than that."

You are mistaken, Daener continued. *The Realms have done nothing for you. For years, you were lost in a perpetual state of drunkenness, of abandonment. For years, you contemplated ending your life for good. We could not allow that to happen. You were valuable then, but you are not now. You have lived only to strengthen the soul, Levi. You have lived so that we can TAKE!*

The swarm of Mediators hissed at their leader's emphatic charge.

I warned you to surrender, hero. I hoped for you to see the truth in things, but it seems that you have refused. You have made your choice. You will watch your home burn to ashes. You will watch the men, women, and children you have come to love die in front of you. You will watch the other Realms succumb to our strength. Only after all that has come to pass, Daener finished, *will we allow you to die.*

A knot of hate filled the center of Levi's chest. He breathed inward, holding the ball of it deep inside.

"Do what you have come here to do," Levi barked. "Go ahead. Take it."

Before Levi's hands could raise in surrender, Daener rushed to face him. With a bundle of claws, the monster pushed through the wall of Levi's chest. A white-blue light burst from the hero in all directions, filling the storm with a tragic sort of glow. Both Levi and Daener screamed, leveling their intensity to match the other. The further Daener pushed, the brighter Levi shone while the hundreds of monsters waiting for their portion dropped to their knees, screaming out.

Take it, Daener screamed. *Take it we shall.*

Then in a matter of seconds, all grew dark.

The rain stopped falling. The air thickened. The moon broke through the shallowing clouds. There were no Mediators, no Daener, no monsters hissing into the violent wind. The sound of the collective thought had rid itself from Levi's head.

All that was left was him—a normal soul.

"Levi?" Corgin called. He had poked his eyes from the side chute of his underground shelter. "Levi! Where did they go?"

Levi stood from his unconscious state and scanned the square. The townsfolk had begun to make their way from their hiding places. No visions plagued him. No untrustworthy thoughts riddled his mind.

"They're gone!" a woman named Hilda screamed. "The Mediators! They're gone!"

Levi, nearly dumbfounded, smiled wholeheartedly for the first time in his life.

"Yes. Yes, they are."

RED AND WHITE

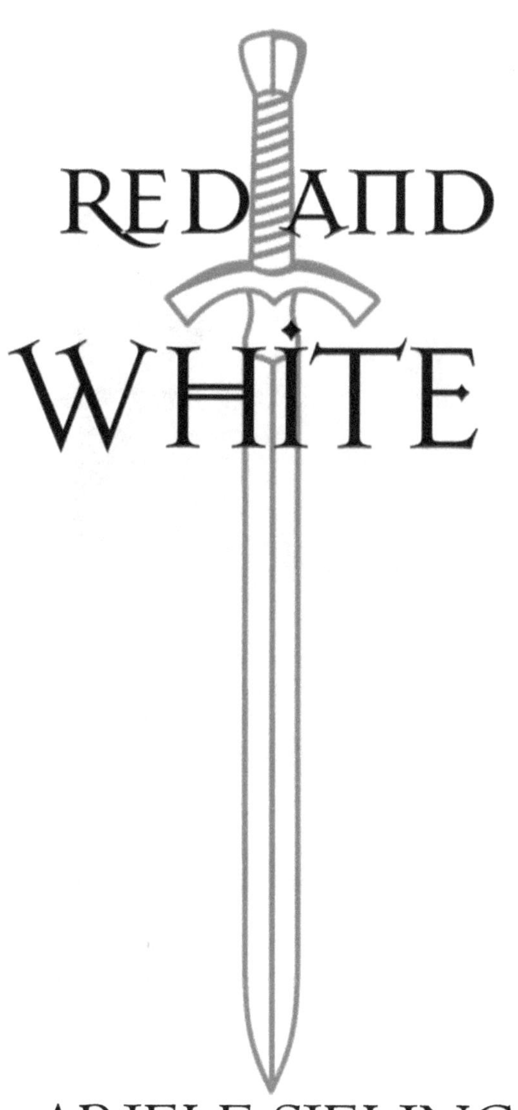

ARIELE SIELING

About Ariele Sieling

Ariele Sieling is the author of the *Sagittan Chronicles*, a science fiction series, and the children's book series, *Rutherford the Unicorn Sheep*, and has had a variety of science fiction and fantasy short stories published in several anthologies. She lives in New Hampshire with her husband and three cats.

She can be found at her website and on Facebook, Goodreads, and

www.arielesieling.com

RED AND WHITE

Yesterday, Red and I did the first really stupid thing we'd done in years: we let in a stray dog. It was frigid outside, the kind of cold that makes the toes fall off birds. We heard a scratching at the door. Red got her gun, but when we looked, it was just a dog; the poor animal was shivering and so skinny we could see his ribs. He could have been a magical weapon of some kind or a shapeshifter sent by the crazy nightlings, but we let him in anyway. Guess it means we're still human.

At any rate, he didn't kill us, just left when the sun came up.

It was a huge surprise when we saw him again the next evening. We went hunting every day, just before nightfall, and without fail he began to show up, night after night after night.

We gave him scraps of food when we could spare them, but we didn't dare name him. It was no use getting too attached.

I always hated food runs. We were, of course, smarter than the roving nightlings, but they had more resources. Endless weapons, endless magic—only the unlucky ones got caught with their heads up their behinds. Those were our favourites—easy to beat, easy to kill.

Sometimes, we scavenged for food down by the river. Fish were always good, if you could cook them without being caught. Watercress and river weed were usually findable, but we had to be careful because we didn't want to overfish or overharvest our food supplies. Luckily, the closest encampment was several miles away, and they rarely ventured into our part of the city. Bloody redheads, they called us.

Our main food supply came from the traps. The nightlings treated us like pests so they would set up food stations where they tried to lure us in. We were good at killing them by now, so often we looked for traps and raided them for food. Ambush the ambushers.

It was during one of these trips that the dog came in handy.

Although we didn't enjoy going out at night, it was often easier to avoid the roving eyes of the nightlings by at least waiting until twilight. We snuck through the decrepit city streets under the dimming light of the setting sun, looking for anything that might indicate a stash of food. After a bit, we came across an old abandoned warehouse in the south end of town. Peeling paint, broken glass, and graffiti slathered on every surface greeted us, but we knew it was more than that: a nightling hid behind a bush.

This nightling was camouflaged—it had changed to green, the color of bushes. Never mind that bushes were dull, dirty grey. Even the brown leaves had long since blown away. We always wondered why they thought this tactic would work. Nightlings look nothing like bushes, especially when they've changed to a different colour.

Red ran ahead to scout, while I got my gear ready: rope, an orbifizer cobbled together from old bits of electronics and charged with magic, a flashlight, a bag of rocks, a slingshot, and some other useful odds and ends. You never know what might come in handy.

I pulled out my sling and a rock, swung it around my head, and let it fly. The rock smashed against the nightling's face, but it didn't seem to notice. Frowning, I took stock of my situation. Maybe it was asleep or enchanted, and I could just overwhelm it. Or maybe it was just learning—pretending. That would be bad.

I slipped forward quietly, pulling out my orbifizer. The orbifizer was a tool designed to give sudden jolts of power, helpful in tasks like starting engines or killing fish mercifully. In this case, it would hopefully overwhelm the nightling's magical capacity and cause it to die. I reached out and zapped the nightling. It blinked once, and then its crackly, inhuman voice intoned: "Not enough magics. Sleeeeep. Sleeeep."

This is always good news—a nightling dying on its own... although, it was unusual for a nightling to be out and about with no friends and not enough power. But before I had any more time to think about it, Red came barreling around the corner on a gigantic warehouse loader, chased by a slew of angry nightlings. Their little wings rapidly fluttered, keeping them in the air. They weren't very fast creatures, but they were persistent.

The thing about our city is that since the calamity, the Creatures had gone to great lengths to take control of everything. After they had annihilated the majority of the humans living here, they rid us of electricity. It was a foreign power to them, and evil. Or something. In its place, they ran conduits from the wells of magic located in extremely secured areas to the other used buildings in the area—the baths, the factories, the houses—you name it.

It was one of these conduits that Red accidentally crashed into with the forklift; one of the forks knocked the power pole over. It crashed forward and a power line came loose, flopping erratically through the air. I ducked and froze, hoping desperately that the power line would miss me. Getting zapped by raw magic is almost certain to be deadly, though low levels are survivable. Red jumped off the loader and it continued on by, still followed by the swarm of angry nightlings. She covered my body with hers, as older sisters do.

Then the power line struck the sleeping nightling. Sparks hissed and fizzed. The blubbery voice intoned, "I is awake… awake!"

Red gulped and I heard her breathing speed up. She would be the first to go. Maybe once she died, the nightling would think it did its job and leave me, cowering under her corpse, to live another day.

"Human detected," the nightling said. "Eradication in progress."

I held my breath.

From nowhere we heard barking. The dog's bark was thin, a little like the sound of pennies in a wooden cup.

The flying black imp of hate turned. "Disturbance detected. Disturbance indicates human location."

Red and I didn't dare to breathe.

The nightling turned and flew off in the direction of the dog. We waited five minutes without moving, but the air was clean and quiet. All nightlings seemed to have disappeared.

When Red finally sat up, she was crying.

"Poor dog," she whispered. "He saved us."

I nodded.

We scrambled to our feet and quickly slid into the building. Our eyes widened. It hadn't been a trap at all. This warehouse was where they stored their human food to put in the traps. It was a jackpot.

It's the kind of thing in a life that makes you want to squeal and dance, but we didn't dare for fear of the nightlings' return. There was still a horde of them out there, searching for us. Quietly we filled up our bags with as much as we could carry, hid more food in other nearby locations, and then carefully snuck back towards home, reveling in our newfound treasure.

When we got home, the dog was sitting on our porch. Red squealed and ran to hug him.

He ate well that night.

We didn't decide to name him until after the next incident.

♦

Food isn't the only thing we need to survive. Clean water, clothes, and medicine all rank pretty high on the list. The river is our primary source of water. Of course, it isn't clean, but we strain it and boil it and have to make do. Occasionally we find a stash of bottled water from the old days and ration that to last for as long as possible. It tastes better, plus, it's already been purified.

The nightlings usually leave the river alone. Water and Creatures don't mix well.

They have to drink it, sure, but they don't like the way it feels, so they stay away. Our guess is that it interferes with magic somehow. That's why they stopped the rain by building a huge dome over the city. They're like the cats, from the old days. But even though they don't like to get wet, every so often they'll send a patrol down to the river to make sure none of us pesky humans are nosing around.

This was one of those days. We were being a little careless, because even when your survival is at stake, it's hard to be vigilant at all hours of day and night. Dusk was falling, and we spent the walk to the river chatting. Our conversations on nights like these varied from talking about the past, to discussing things we had read about in books. Today we were trying to figure out the purpose of social conventions like marriage. It can be difficult to understand what they were for when you have no social context for them.

I had a vague recollection of attending a wedding—I think it was one of our uncle's. The bride wore a white dress, the groom had a flower on his shirt. We didn't have flowers any more. I mostly remember wearing a pretty yellow dress though, and that I didn't like my shoes.

Red said Mom and Dad were married, but I don't remember either of them very well, so it still doesn't mean much. They had matching rings, apparently some kind of symbol for marriage. Red and I each wear one around our necks. I have Dad's.

It had rained outside the city the night before, so the river was high and rushing fast. We noticed an odd thing, though—a big chunk of metal had washed down and was stuck on some rocks. We wandered down to see what it was and then froze. A nightling was stuck in the mud in the shallow part of the creek on the other side of the metal sheet. It was struggling and grunting, and overall did not look too happy.

It saw us, too. Of course. That's what always happens.

"Humanses!" it yelled as it started shooting bursts of magic at us.

Red grabbed me and we ducked behind the big piece of metal blocking the flow of water.

"Let's flush it out," Red whispered to me.

We carefully positioned ourselves, grabbing tightly to the metal sheet, and with all of our strength, heaved! The sheet came loose from the rocks and we tossed it towards shore, bracing ourselves as a deluge rushed around us.

When we surfaced, the nightling was gone, presumably drowned or far downstream and steaming mad.

"Awesome," Red said, grinning. She trudged out of the river, dripping.

Then, from nowhere the dog flew in, barking like mad.

I spun around and so did Red; we saw the nightling hovering nearby, shaking droplets from its head and hair, and scowling a violently angry scowl.

"Humanses," it intoned.

Red shrieked. It seemed that we hadn't drowned it, but freed it. Dog kept running, passed right by us, and just before he hit the river, leaped, grabbing the creature's wing in his teeth. The two spun sideways, crashing into the water. I didn't hesitate, but jumped in too, looking for Dog. There were bubbles and the current was strong. I felt like I was under forever, with the dark waters swirling around me. Then my hands touched fur, and I wrapped my arms around Dog and kicked my way to the surface.

He coughed and wheezed and threw up a little, but he was fine, eventually. Red hovered over us, pointing her gun and an extremely angry expression at the river, guarding us should the nightling decide to resurface. It didn't, and after Dog was feeling a little better, we quickly filled our jugs and headed back towards home.

We let Dog in again that evening, covered him with blankets, and even started a little fire. His tail wagged and he seemed to smile, but he left again before morning.

"Weird dog," Red said. "But I love him already."

I agreed.

We decided to name him, but just Dog. A name, but not too much, in case we really did lose him.

The last couple of weeks had been hard, but we were in better shape than we had ever been. Water, plenty of food, and our new dog made life just a little bit easier. But of course, it doesn't usually stay like that. When one problem goes away, another one fills in its place. It's like Tetris, this game Red and I used to play on an old game console, before it died.

Pieces fall from the top of the screen to fill up the bottom, and you have to organize them to make them go away. But the pieces never stop falling. They keep coming, one after another, faster and faster, until you inevitably lose. In real life, losing meant dying.

The next day, the power went out. Power was something we always had. The Creatures needed it to power their systems, to refill their magical reservoir. We tapped into their grid, enabling us to heat our living quarters, charge our flashlights and lamps, and occasionally take a hot bath. We always had back-up systems, of course—a battery operated pellet stove for heat, solar flashlights for light—but since electricity had been banned, having access to their power supply made survival hugely easier.

"Either the whole pool ran out," Red began plotting through our course of action, "a conduit fell over, or they found our tap and cut it. If that's the case, it means they can follow it directly here. We need to get out immediately and figure out what's going on. Grab the emergency packs and let's go."

"It's already dark," I argued. "We'll freeze out there, if the nightlings and their night vision don't spot us first!"

"We've got night vision too," Red argued, "even if only one of us can use it. I don't see that we have any other choices."

"Should we go to a different hideout?" I asked.

"No, because our power tap runs to those places, too." She shook her head. "I'm afraid we're on the streets until we figure out what's going on. Bundle up."

I nodded. She was right, as usual. Survival first, then comfort. I wondered where she had learned all this, but in our world, experience makes you either a pro or dead. She was still alive, so that meant she was a master in survival—and I was just lucky to have her.

We put on three layers of socks, heavy pants, and winter boots. On top, we wore fitted convection thermal shirts, which were lightweight but still able to keep us warm. Gloves were also a necessity, and hats to hide our bright red hair. Then, Red pulled out the magic-proof vests. We never wore these, as they were heavy, limited movement, and not guaranteed to work. We had found them on a raid several years back, and taken them just in case.

"You think?" I asked.

"It can't hurt," Red replied. "We'll have to move slowly anyway, and if we get caught, we're probably dead. At least with these we could get hit and only pretend to die. There are likely to be swarms of nightlings out tonight, so I think every precaution is warranted."

I nodded and slipped mine on over my head. It was bulkier than I remembered, but still fitted. They were the new kind built just before the Creature uprising by SorcererTech. We were convinced that SorcererTech was responsible for the apocalypse, but at least they had left a few useful things lying around.

The last thing Red grabbed was her sword. A sword, like many other things lying around an abandoned city, was the least useful weapon against flying nightlings who could shoot us with magic. But it was ours. Our father had purchased it on a business trip overseas, and brought it home. We had oohed and ahhed over the shiny metal weapon, and he had hung it on the wall in his study like a trophy. When we first escaped from the Creatures, it was the first weapon we grabbed, and we still had it with us to remind us that we would survive no matter what.

We heaved our emergency packs, filled with things like flashlights, food, water, weapons, blankets, knives, and matches, onto our shoulders and headed quietly into the street. There were no street lamps—there never were—or lights of any kind. Humans had to be careful or the Creatures would kill us and use our bodies as fertilizer for growing their food. At least, that's what the stories said. Most likely they'd just kill us and leave our bodies to rot in the streets. Our windows were boarded up with blackout curtains we had raided from an old furnishings store.

The light of the setting sun made the shadows long and deep, but there was still enough light for us to pick our way carefully away from our home. Twilight was always a strange hour, and tales told of animals transforming into humans, of Creatures transforming into night terrors, and of untold murder and mayhem. We never left the house at this hour, and the tingling sensation in my hands and stomach were indication enough for me that we needed to find someplace to hide, and fast.

"Shouldn't we be going in the opposite direction from the magic pool?" I whispered.

"No," Red replied. "It's more important that we find out what's going on."

Red had been raising me for so long. I believed everything she said. But this time, I was starting to doubt.

"Are you sure?" I asked. "Couldn't we hide and then find out in the morning?"

"What if they ransack our house?" she said. "If we're in hiding, we won't know and they'll be on the hunt for us. It won't be any safer then than now."

"What about the stories?" I pushed. "The animals, the murder…"

"Just stories!" Red insisted. "Stories that people tell to make themselves feel better, to entertain each other, to keep children inside at night. Nothing to worry about."

I nodded silently, but swallowed deeply. I wasn't convinced.

The evening was quiet. The only noises were from far away machinery and the bubbling of the river as it rushed from one end of the city to the other. We moved softly through the streets, looking for a glimpse of light and listening for the blubbery hissing of nightlings. Anytime Red heard a noise she didn't recognize she would stop, hunch down, and wait. I always hated this, because without moving, it was so cold.

A half mile from home, she froze, gesturing for me to get down. Slowly and surely, she pulled a gun from her belt and pointed it in front of us, taking a deep breath.

That's when I heard the noise. I didn't know how she could have heard it earlier; it sounded like a very quiet click, click, click, on the pavement. I covered my head with my hands, waiting for a shot or a noise or a command.

I was surprised when instead of any of those things, I heard a laugh. In the middle of a dangerous mission, Red laughed.

Looking up, a smile spread over my face. It was just Dog, and he was wagging his tail and panting at us.

"You shouldn't be here," Red said to him. "I can't protect you."

We both petted him for a moment. He didn't seem to care about her warnings, because as soon as we started moving again, he followed. We went another quarter of a mile before Red pulled a blanket from her pack, ripped it into smaller pieces, and tied it around his feet. The clicking noise of his toenails on cement would attract any nightling within hearing.

I don't know how long we walked, but it felt like forever and all traces of the sun had completely vanished from the sky when we met the first nightling. It didn't see us, but flew right past, focused on whatever errand it was on.

The next nightling flew past us two minutes after the first, similarly focused. It seemed unlikely that much time would pass before we ran into patrolling nightlings that wanted nothing more than to slice our poor internal organs from our bodies and leave our rotting carcasses on the pavement. Or take them back to their greenhouses.

We had seen more than a few rotting human carcasses in our time on the streets, and I always told Red that if I died she should dump me in the river or burn my corpse. The thought of my end being so vile and irreverent had caused many sleepless nights. And I certainly didn't want to become fertilizer. I promised Red I would do the same thing for her, and even though we were already biological sisters, we made it a blood-sealed promise.

The next nightling was on patrol. We froze, hidden in the shadows, and waited for it to pass. Dog didn't move or make a sound. He clearly understood the intensity of the situation. I had never met a dog before, but I had never imagined they would be this smart.

After the patrol nightling strolled away, Red peered around the corner of the next building, before ducking back hurriedly.

"There are dozens," she whispered, "and they're not at the power grid. They're around the Alonso House."

The Alonso House was where we had made our first home, which had subsequently been invaded by Creatures. That was when we were small. Mom and Dad had died in the attack, but the Creatures hadn't found Red and me hiding in the closet upstairs. We waited for nearly two days before sneaking out, and had barely made it to our next temporary home without being killed. But we were both survivors.

"Do you think they're after us?" I asked.

"I don't know," Red replied.

"Did we ever run power to that house?" I continued. If we did, that would explain why they were there.

Red nodded slowly, whispering, "Back when I thought we would be able to live at home. Back before I knew how the nightlings picked what houses to invade."

We looked at each other for a long moment. This meant that they had likely found the power tap that led to all of our safe places. This meant that there was no telling how long we would be without power. Our only real choice was to run—to find a new place to live and a new way to steal magic.

"But where?" I asked, voicing our biggest fear. This had been a repeated topic of discussion over the years, and one that never had a satisfactory answer. In the North, the Regal Clan reigned, a family of humans that had managed to occupy the same territory for many years. They raided and stole from the Creatures like we did, but were at constant war with clans in the same neighborhood. We had managed to find relative peace on our own.

To the West lay the factories, where the Creatures gave birth to new kinds of nightlings designed to do new and different things. Rumor had it that top level sorcerers from SorcererTech and their families still lived among the Creatures, and continued to help them improve and learn to better use magic. If this was true, it may have actually been humans that had brought the end of the world.

If we headed too much further South, over the river, the dome ended and we would have to trek out into the wilderness where the wolves cried and the clouds rained. Neither of us knew how to survive outside—we hadn't ever seen a wolf before. I imagined them to look like grotesque versions of the nightlings, with huge wings and claws, terrifying faces, and noses that breathed fire.

The problem with the East was the mystery. We knew almost nothing about it. We had never met a human that came from that direction. A huge wall separated our side of the city from the East; to get through it you had to squeeze through sewer lines or climb over the top. We knew where to go, but not what lay waiting for us.

Red shook her head. She didn't have any idea what to tell me. She didn't know what the best decision would be—for the first time, she didn't know what to do.

We sat there for a while, staring at each other and contemplating our predicament. Dog sat patiently between us, looking back and forth and wagging his tail. Any minute now the nightlings would arrive. Any minute now we would get up and leave… or die.

"The East," Red finally said. "Let's go East. The Regals will never let us into their clan, except possibly as slaves. We can't deal with the Creatures in the West, and I'd rather save the outside as our last option. We go East."

I nodded, swallowing. Often I had dreamed of the other side of the wall being a place of safety, with real beds and warm fireplaces, princes and crowns and warm food. But in reality, it was probably more like this side—filled with death, fear, and destruction.

We slowly stood and backed silently away from the street where the nightlings patrolled, keeping to the shadows and making an extra effort not to make any noise.

"We should avoid any of our other safe houses, too," Red whispered to me, taking a right on Elm Street.

That meant a very long and winding path to the East Wall, but I had no doubt we could make it there. It was what lay on the other side that I was worried about now. Dog kept close to my heels, padding silently down the streets.

If nothing else, he was a comfort, a reminder that Creatures weren't the only thing that make up the world, and that in addition to evil, there was also good lurking somewhere.

Butternut Street, Visor Lane, cut behind house number 451 and onto Lumberjack Place. Head South towards Evening Road and then weave through the Warehouse District. It was the dead of night; in fact, in only a short time, the sun would begin to come back up. It was the kind of darkness where you can see more light behind your eyelids than when your eyes are open.

An hour later, after an extremely circuitous route, the first grey light of the sun began to make the world around us a little more navigable. We were nearly to our destination, so it seemed fitting that we would run into trouble. Red, moving more quickly than ever, turned onto Rover Street. This was parallel to the one that ran along the East Wall. Almost running now, we hurried across the street, when Red came to an abrupt stop.

I couldn't believe we hadn't seen it.

A camouflaged nightling hid behind a bush. It was bright green. It blinked at us and announced loudly, "Humanses. I can hear thems."

Red began to back up slowly. Maybe if the nightling hadn't seen us, we could hide.

Then from nowhere a sea of squishy, flying nightlings descended, surrounding us. They moved closer and closer. Together, they made a humming noise that I had heard many times before at a distance, but which was much more terrifying up close. Their skin glinted as the rays of the sun peeked over the rim of the planet and reflected off the bottom of the dome. The deep blue colour of their skin made them difficult to see in the morning light, and had it been completely dark, they would have been nearly impossible to see.

I was so afraid, I was paralyzed. I couldn't even breathe. I kept saying in my head, "it's not the end, it's not the end," but I didn't believe a word of it. Then, Red reached out and dragged me to the ground. She threw her body over me and squeezed her eyes shut.

"Love you, sis," she whispered.

"I love you too," I whispered back.

"You know what to do."

I nodded. My job in this situation was to survive and get away. Then I would come back and dump Red's body in the river. I would not let her end up like the rest of the bodies in the city. Or as fertilizer. I would not.

It's hard to say what happened next, because sometimes life just doesn't make any sense. We were lying on the ground, Red covering my body with hers. A horde of angry nightlings—though "horde" in this case probably only meant ten or fifteen, but it felt like dozens—looked down forebodingly with their magic guns at the ready, and Dog whimpered next to us.

A nightling fired at us, and I heard some coughing and shouting. I was afraid Dog had been hit—he started to seize, shaking back and forth and whimpering. I blinked and then a man stood over us, with Red's sword in hand. He swung it around, knocking the nightlings off balance. They started to scream, "Humanses attacking! Attack back!" The sword pierced right through the soft belly of one nightling and it fell to the ground, smoking. Another nightling got smacked by the wide side of the blade and it went spinning, crashing into a pole.

The others began to shoot, streams of magic lighting up the night around us. I pulled my gun from my holster and began to shoot back from my awkward position under my sister, trying desperately not to hit the man that protected us. It was so loud, and there was so much noise and smoke. The nightlings yelled at us, telling us to die. They called for backup by shooting coloured flares into the night sky. I prayed silently that we would escape before the bigger Creatures came. There was no way we could survive them. The nightlings crashed to the earth in little explosions around us. The dirt and grime from the ground and the blue blood from the nightlings got in my hair and my eyes. It smelled of sulfur. Red's body weighed heavily on mine, but she was my hope, my future. The vest would protect her and we would flee East together.

The next moment, it was silent. All I could hear was the breathing of the man standing over us and the hissing of a nearby dying nightling. When I opened my eyes, the man had bent down and was lifting Red off of me. Her eyes were open.

"Red?" I said.

She didn't respond, didn't move, didn't blink.

She didn't blink.

"Red?" I said again.

The man reached out and took my hand, shaking his head.

"No!" I shouted. "No! It wasn't supposed to happen this way!" But was that true? Wasn't that the plan all along? Red's life goal was to raise me, to protect me, to give me a chance to live.

"I don't want it," I whispered, throwing myself over her and hugging her body. "I don't want a chance to live if it means living without you."

"White." The man reached down and touched my arm. His voice was deep, husky. It sounded familiar. "Let me carry her out of sight, in case more Creatures come."

I swallowed and nodded, tears streaming down my face. At least I didn't have to drag her. At least his presence spared her that indignity. I reached out and closed her eyes.

He bent down to lift her and I saw that he was naked, except for a few pieces of cloth wrapped around his waist. Red's body was limp, lifeless. The tears wouldn't stop. I didn't think I could live without her. The things she did for me—the hunting, the finding, the protecting—I didn't know how she did them. I couldn't possibly do them for myself.

"Who are you?" I asked, the tears an endless stream.

"I'm Dog," he replied, turning to look at me. "I've been here all along."

"But…" If he was Dog, that meant he had turned into a human.

"A werewolf," he said simply, "but I promise I won't hurt you."

What would Red do? Would she trust him? A Dog that was also a human? I needed her. I couldn't make these decisions. She had been there for so long and given me so much.

The talking. The laughing. The whispered conversations and imaginary friends. The plotting and planning, the stealing and raiding. The arguments and disagreements. The first nightling we ever killed. The first fish we ever caught. She was my whole universe. What was left?

I followed Dog into the alleyway and he set her gently on the ground, propping up her head on her backpack. Still not safe, Red would say, but probably okay for a few minutes. I reached down and touched the wound that had killed her. Blood poured everywhere. I pulled back her shirt—she wasn't wearing a vest. I pulled open my shirt and yanked at my own vest. She had stuck them together—I was wearing both.

More tears streamed down my face. How could she do this to me? How dare she leave me like this?

"What do you want to do with the body?" Dog asked. "We can't wait much longer."

"Bury it." I shook my head. "Burn it. Throw it in the river."

I reached down and gently lifted the necklace with my mother's ring from Red's neck and placed it around my own neck. What would Red do if it were me lying lifeless in the street? "Burn."

The man nodded and stood.

"Wait," I said. "Take some clothes."

He looked at me and smiled sadly. "I have some. Just wait."

I waited, wondering if she could feel anything. Did it hurt when she died? Had she been thinking of me? Had she been thinking of our mother? Of our father? Was she still out there somewhere? Or was she really gone forever? Did it matter? To me, she was dead.

I didn't notice I was sobbing until I couldn't breathe. Gasps wracked my body and a river of tears poured down my face. I had to burn her, had to leave her body safe from the torments of death. I hoped, deep inside, that the whole city burned, as penance for the death of my sister. Every Creature destroyed. Every human that didn't work to protect her left only as burning flesh. Every house and building and stream—gone.

When the man returned, he was fully clothed and carried a pack and a gun, as well as two cans of gasoline. I began to take deep breaths, conscious that I needed to be able to help, to be a useful companion and not incapacitated by grief. Red would be mad if I died because I was careless while grieving for her. Especially since she gave her own life to save mine.

I laid her body in a straight line in the center of the alleyway and crossed her arms over her chest. Then, I kissed her forehead, leaking more tears onto her face, and reached out to take one of the cans of gasoline.

I poured one can over her body, from her head to her toes, and soaked her clothes with as much as I could. I took the other can and drew a circle around it with the liquid, and then lines over to the buildings on each side of her. I wanted it all to burn. If I could get two buildings on fire, that would be a good start.

I hoped that the nightlings sent to put out the fire would take a long time to arrive, and that the fire would spread out of control. Part of me hoped that I, too, would die in flames. We stepped back towards the East Wall—Red had been so close to freedom! —and looked back at Red's body. Dog took her pack and began to stuff it through the pipe that used to carry water from one side of the wall to the other. It was empty now—no rain, no people.

With my head bowed, tears still pouring from my eyes, I lit a match.

"Goodbye, sister," I whispered, as I tossed it forward, and watched my whole world go up in flames.

The heat seared the skin on my face as I stepped back, away from the fire, away from my home, away from Red.

Then, Dog grabbed my hand and we crawled through the tunnel to the East.

I wanted to scream, wanted to yell, wanted to sob. Wanted to throw my body into the flames and be with her. But she died for me. The least I could do was live.

Amphibian Anthologies

Out of the Darkness was just the beginning! Check out our upcoming anthologies below!

Surrender to Passion
Romance

Beamed Up
Science Fiction

CROSSBONES
Pirates

SWITCHING GEARS
Steampunk

DUDES IN DISTRESS
Romance